The Third Generation Series

Book 5

Wanda: A New Life – Hidden Secrets

by

Margaret Gregory

Tried and Trusted Indie Publishing

Also by Margaret Gregory
TYMOREAN TRUST SERIES:
Book 1 - Power Rising
Book 2 - Great Ones
Book 3 - The Return to Earth
Book 4 – Earth Mission
Book 5 – Alien Contact
Book 6 - Invasion

ATAPI SORCERESS SERIES:
Prequel – Korvu: The Beginning
Book 1- The Wild One
Book 2 – Atapi Sorceress

THE THIRD GENERATION SERIES:
Wanda: From Bad to Worse
Wanda: Choosing Crime
Wanda – Early Days (anthology) Book 1 and 2
Wanda – Risking Life to Live
Erin: The Forcing of Wisdom

Tried and Trusted Indie Publishing
PO Box 2728
Rowville, Vic. 3178 Australia
www.tatindiepublishing.com / triedandtrustedindie@gmail.com

Wanda: A New Life
Part One – Hidden Secrets

Chapter 1

The Defence Department Facility at Rockwater was an extensive establishment amongst the foothills of the San Gabriel Mountains and about seventy-five miles from Los Angeles. It served many functions, being used mainly as a training and evaluation centre for government agents. It was also used for convalescing agents as it had its own hospital and research centre. On rarer occasions, it was used as a detention centre.

Wanda Martin hadn't quite worked out which category her presence fitted into. By rights, she could have been thrown in jail for twenty years or more. Since, for about six years, she had been performing lucrative break-ins for organised crime boss Harrison Franklin. She had been his top agent, but she had turned on him and helped put him and his two sons in prison.

Technically, she was in the witness protection program, even though certain parties had convinced the crime boss that she was dead. It hadn't been hard, because at the time of the trial she had been battling a recurrence of a chronic genetic disorder, and had in fact come close to dying. She was still trying to get back to top fitness.

Then, the parties that had made her seem to be dead, had recruited her to do hush-hush stuff for the government. The people in the Government that had to okay that were antagonistic. They didn't doubt her skills, just her – well morals or ethics or what ever. They wanted to be sure she would limit her "crimes" to what she was told to do – and not go to work for herself.

Of course, having her claim that it was the thrill of danger and the associated adrenalin rush that had made her a criminal had not helped them be sure of her mental state. The powers wanted her 'evaluated'. At least, Jim Phillips, her new 'handler' or 'boss' or what ever the jargon was, knew that it had been her way of fighting her chronic problem.

So, Rockwater was her home for the while. She wasn't going to be sent to prison, but she wasn't strictly free. That was something she could live with for now – even though sometimes it irked. There were some restrictions on her movements. Officially, it wasn't like a prison sentence. She had not had anything added to her criminal record. However, she had overheard one of the powers call it – 'six months precautionary detention'. Or had she heard the man think it? She wasn't sure. It meant that she was not allowed to leave the base, but she had free access to much of the base and nothing to prevent her from making use of the facilities.

It also allowed the various 'shrinks' and others to find her for evaluation purposes. At least she had the base psychologist firmly on her side. He had examined her when she had first arrived and listened to her own summation of the compulsions that drove her. He had since told her that his own observations agreed with her comments.

Even so, it was hard for some people to be convinced that she could be trusted. Only someone that really knew her could comprehend and understand the method in her apparent madness. Or that the compulsions that drove her were not devised in the mind of an irresponsible child.

Wanda privately decided that the 'detention' was meant as a test of her 'obedience'. The implication being, step out of line once and you will go to prison. She didn't want to step out of line. The types of work Jim Phillips wanted to use her for, excited her. She couldn't wait – but she had to.

A new identity and a new life – that's what she had now. And once they had finished their comprehensive psychological tests, and their exhaustive security checks – she could get on with it.

In the meantime, she was slowly getting herself to the peak of fitness, and enjoying being Mrs David Martin. She and her new husband had the use of one of the small cottages on the base. So while all her movements outside of the cottage were noted and recorded, the space within the cottage was her private unmonitored refuge.

While David was off doing secret stuff with Jim Phillips, Wanda consoled herself with knowing that her turn would come to use her 'talents' for her country. Jim didn't have any doubts that she would be cleared to work for him. He trusted her with a great deal of the organisational details of his work.

When she was not needed for that, she threw herself into her personal training program. Working out in the gymnasium when no one else was around, observing the activities of others on the base to strengthen her ability to notice and recall details, learning new languages, and generally training herself to be an undercover agent. One of Jim's best. She practiced the unlawful art of opening locks when the occasion permitted – to keep those skills sharp – but never anywhere near restricted areas.

Dr Paul Matheson, temporarily in charge of the Rockwater base, did not know Wanda well. Nor was he impressed by her. Two days ago, he had found her performing dare-devil manoeuvres in the two storey part of the gymnasium. She had remained unimpressed by his rendition of the riot act. When he had finished, she had factually pointed out that he had no authority to prevent her from using the gymnasium. She declined to add that she was simply copying 'stunts' that certain select members of the defence department performed as part of their training.

That confrontation was still in Matheson's mind. Wanda sensed it and it may have been the cause of his unwillingness to listen to her now.

This time, Wanda was in the wrong and she knew it. If Matheson wasn't being so pig-headed, she would willingly admit it. If Matheson had listened to her in the first place – or if David had been there – she wouldn't have gone off and proven how easy it was to get out of the base unnoticed.

"I did ask to be accompanied," Wanda pointed out in a very reasonable voice. She shook off the grip of the two guards that had bodily marched her into the director's office. She seemed to have anticipated the tirade Matheson then unleashed.

"Why did you attempt to leave? You are officially restricted to the base. This action of yours will be reported to the highest levels and may mean the rescinding of your pardon and reinstatement of criminal charges."

"I told you…why I wanted to be accompanied," Wanda reminded him. "But you didn't consider it important that two men appear to be keeping the base under observation. I for one, wanted to know why."

"I sent out two men. Two of the best. They found no one," Matheson told her severely.

"The same men are still in the place I specified two hours ago," Wanda insisted, still holding her anger in check. "What are you going to do about it?"

"I have your report. I have taken appropriate action," Matheson told her coldly. "The matter is now out of your hands. You will take no further unauthorised action."

Wanda glared at him. "It's your hide," she snapped.

Matheson clearly didn't appreciate her retort.

"This matter will be reported," he told her. "You may go!"

Wanda pushed past the guards that had accompanied her from the gate and stalked from the room.

"David!" Wanda interrupted her husband's remonstrations. "I am a big girl. I knew what I was doing. And I don't need to be reminded of what is at stake. Matheson deserves to be getting a right dressing down. It is not because they think I tried to get out. It's because he was being a pig-headed idiot. I told him there were men up there acting suspiciously. I told him exactly where they were. He ignored my information. Eventually sent out two men, who went no where near where I said, and were spotted by the two watchers."

"Calm down," David told his wife, as he dropped into an adjacent chair. "They are taking the proper steps now."

"Now!" Wanda snapped up straight, eyes flashing. "Matheson could have had those men in custody now. Instead, they are probably half way around the world with..."

"With what?" David asked. "What is the matter with you?"

"It's arguing with Matheson," Wanda claimed, forcing herself to calm down and relax back into the chair. "I have had an appalling headache all day and that didn't help."

"That's not all," David commented thoughtfully. "You are as twitchy as a spooked horse. What are you afraid of? Matheson's threat to have your pardon revoked?"

"No. He hasn't the authority. And if General Addison is treating my report seriously, there won't be trouble."

"So what is it?" David insisted. "Something is troubling you. I can tell. I know you. Take a good look at yourself!"

Wanda shook her head as if to deny anything was bothering her, and then stopped still. "You are right, Dav. I haven't been able to think straight with this headache. I feel...felt...that somewhere out there," Wanda pointed towards the higher mountains, "someone was terrified – needed help."

"So that's why you took off," David murmured, understanding. "I assume Elisabeth is alive and well in LA?"

"What?" Wanda asked, her attention returning to David.

"Elisabeth? Your sister? Is OK?" David spelled it out.

"Yeah. I called her earlier. She's fine. Oh! It feels like it would if Lisbeth was in trouble. How odd." Wanda seemed to be considering something.

David reached over and began to gently massage Wanda's temples. After a few minutes, Wanda pushed his hands away, and used her hand to cover her mouth. David gently pulled it away.

"What is it?"

"David, don't ask me how I know, but whoever I sensed before, is still up there, is still terrified and still needs help."

"I think we need to tell someone," David suggested softly. "What haven't you told me?"

If asked, he would say he had absolutely no ESP. But he knew Wanda and knew she often 'just knew' things. He respected that ability, whatever it was.

"Your two missing Russians," Wanda said very softly.

David stiffened. He had not even told her about his last mission. Or the reason why he had been delayed getting back.

"Go on," he urged.

"They are up there. The girl – she's the one who has been giving me the headache. She's hurt, terrified and hungry. She's aware of the people looking for her. Russian agents, not American. She must have been broadcasting her fears before, mentally wanting help. She's not doing it now, perhaps she's asleep. For a while this afternoon, it was all I could do to refrain from proving to Matheson and everyone else that this place is not escape proof and not intrusion proof. I had a picture of this place, through the girl's eyes. She also saw the men. That's when I got the field glasses out and spotted them from here. I reported it to Matheson, and he did nothing. Said it was nothing worth wasting the guards' time on. I asked to be accompanied, to check it out. He didn't exactly laugh at me, but told me I was not allowed to go out."

David hid a faint smile. "So what did you find?'

Wanda laughed. Her husband knew her too well.

"The men had moved, but they had been there for a while. I found several cigarette butts, and I would bet they were foreign. I didn't stay long. I just wanted to be sure I was right. I went back to the base and came in at the gate. The guards didn't think it odd that they hadn't seen me go out. I tried to get them to come back with me but they reported to Matheson."

"Who sent a bullet off reporting your insubordination, and Jim got a please explain, and he spoke to General Addison who flew straight back with me…" David made Wanda grin. "I will need to talk to Jim, but we need to tell this to the General."

"If I told him how I knew – he wouldn't believe me," Wanda protested. "Jim would. Let him tell the General."

"I think we should help look for them as soon as we can," David told her, and Wanda didn't disagree. It was just that her knack for 'just knowing' things tended to freak some people, and be flatly disbelieved by others. "The General is on your side and he can authorise you to go off base."

"Just as long as he doesn't report where he got his tip off from," Wanda muttered. "I know that officious assistant to the Secretary of State doesn't like me. If he hears how I 'just know' things that I have no right knowing, he'll never authorise a security clearance for me."

"Forget him!" David told her. "Do you know where they are? The Professor and his daughter?"

"In a cave," Wanda knew. "I can't pinpoint it. I am not receiving anything from the girl at the moment. I can take you to the place where I saw the watchers. I can probably locate the place where the girl saw the base from. We might be able to track them from there."

"Come on, let's talk to the General. I wonder if any of the guards are trackers," David pulled Wanda to her feet. "We ought to go out while there is still some light left."

Chapter 2

General Addison might have given Wanda a thoughtful look, but he acted on her "knowledge". He admitted to having to prepare more search teams to look for the missing plane that the Russians had been on. Those teams had just left, but he believed in being thorough.

"You can leave as soon as Colonel Aldrin arrives," he told them. "He'll be here within half an hour. The cars are assembling by the east gate."

Wanda and David went back to their cottage for hiking clothes, and to grab some of their own gear.

"Who is that Aldrin fellow?" Wanda asked David.

"Works for the OSI," David told her. "He met us when we got back. Some of his colleagues were taking the Russians to Washington. Jim and I were about to leave to come here when we got word that they had lost contact with the plane. Addison got dragged out of a high level meeting and spotted us at the airport and asked us to hang around."

"Where do they think it went down?" Wanda asked.

"It could be near here – the base is with in the search area. That's why Addison is involved. That and the State Department angle." David dragged on his hiking boots.

"I don't think the Russians could have walked far – not if they are hurt," Wanda considered. "When did they go down?"

David checked his watch. "The plane left at ten, they lost contact soon after take-off, so about six hours ago."

"So how did the Russian agents get here so fast?" Wanda asked aloud.

"That question is being considered by others. We shouldn't be involved," David commented.

"They should have brought those Russians here," Wanda said. "Don't you think?"

"Well, I think that was the original plan," David admitted. "However, I think someone in Washington overruled that idea."

While Wanda walked with David to the gate she wondered if the Russian agents were around because they knew the defectors were meant to come there. She was guessing, though. Because, if the change was a last minute thing, how would the Russians get a bomb or something on the plane to bring it down? Unless they had some directed electronic thing to upset the plane's electronics.

The approach of an army helicopter distracted her. She watched it land over on the base helipad. One passenger disembarked, ducked under the rotor air blast as the helicopter took off again.

The tall man wasn't in uniform, but he had that military look. An upright walk, hair cut short. He greeted Addison, spotted David and nodded his recognition and listened to the planned search. He glanced up at the mountains, and then came over to David.

"David Martin isn't it," he asked, smiling at David and including Wanda.

David nodded. "My wife, Wanda," he introduced.

Aldrin grinned and shook hands with her. "I'm told you spotted watchers here and that you think they are Russian."

Wanda nodded warily. Addison was listening. "I can take you there – it only took me half an hour to walk from here." Addison's expression didn't change.

"Can you show me from here?" Aldrin asked.

Wanda pointed in the direction and described the features she had memorised to pinpoint it.

"Is there a track near there, General?" Aldrin asked.

"Hiking track, not vehicle. The nearest road is about half a mile north."

"Okay, we'll walk from here. Have the cars taken as close as possible," Aldrin directed.

Wanda led the small search group out of the gate and in the direction she had taken earlier. Apart from Aldrin, David and herself, there were three of the base guards. Within half an hour, Wanda stopped at the place where the men had been. Aldrin began to study the ground; Wanda moved to get a view of the base, so she could estimate where the girl must have been. It would have been quite close.

"Good work, Mrs Martin," Aldrin praised. "Have you any other information that might help us. I have found tracks heading south."

Wanda looked at Aldrin and decided to trust him. "This may sound odd, but I know the girl is close. She and her father are hiding. Some kind of cave or gap between rocks. I know, she saw the two watchers, and I know she saw the base. I think, though, that south is the right direction."

Aldrin nodded and led the way. Wanda glanced around as she moved, looking for clues. One of the guards spotted drying blood on some leaves. Wanda saw some bright yellow strands a bit higher. They looked like hair.

"There," she pointed. "David, what colour hair does the girl have?"

David grimaced. "Punk yellow and pink. It was gelled into thick points when we picked her up. She's also into punk make up."

Wanda had a picture of a woman with blue eyes, surrounded by black make up to make both eyes looked bruised. The hair was in stipes of hot pink and yellow.

"Face piercing?" Wanda asked.

"No, none of that," David told her.

"It shouldn't be too hard to pick her out," Wanda said dryly.

"If she's smart – and I am not convinced either way – she will keep the beret on that we gave her. Having to go and get that baggage almost blew the mission. She was quite happy to stay and let the old man go. But our contacts there warned us that the police were watching her too. The Professor's wife had been arrested about a month ago."

"Couldn't you get her too?" Wanda felt the urge to ask.

David shook his head. "We were too late by about a week."

"Oh," Wanda said very softly. She understood that the woman was dead.

They followed Aldrin and the guards for about an hour before they stopped and looked around. They had reached a point where the rocks were taking over from the grasslands. There was still a fair bit of vegetation to interfere with a clear view.

Wanda glanced down and looked for the base. She knew roughly where to look. She compared this view with the one in her mind.

"Which way do you suggest now, Mrs Martin?" Aldrin asked softly. She hadn't heard him approach.

"You can call me Wanda. And, a bit more south east."

"What are you basing your suggestion on?" Aldrin asked. He did not sound sceptical, merely interested.

"I have a picture in my head. In it, I can see a bit of the base and the taller buildings of a town. I think it's Wetherby. To see that, I think we need to be higher."

They moved as she suggested, quietly so that they could hear any noises made by other creatures, though the native creatures were silent. Aldrin gestured for David and one of the guards to move a short distance to his left and the other two guards to move to his right. They had reached a trail in a narrow valley.

David spotted the blood stains on the rock. It looked as if someone had needed to sit down for a while. They concentrated on the area around, but found nothing of use. They went back to the three line search, and this time Aldrin spotted the ground out cigarette butt.

"Looks the same as the others," Wanda said and Aldrin nodded agreement.

Aldrin glanced at his watch, "We've probably only got an hour of light left. This trail is getting rougher. If you were a stranger, in this terrain, with an injured friend, with night coming on – what would you do?"

It sounded like a rhetorical question, but Wanda answered. "Find shelter, is the obvious thing. But, I am sure the woman knows they are being followed by people who probably want them back in Russia. So, I'd say, if I were her, I'd try to find a place to shelter in for the night that was well hidden. I'd want water nearby, but she won't know where to find that except by chance. But, it all depends on how hurt they are."

"Yes," Aldrin agreed. They had just started moving again when Wanda heard a faint whistle – a bit like a bird, but no bird trilled in that way. She stopped at the same time as Aldrin. He put a hand to his ear and seemed to be listening.

"Your David and the guard have spotted movement," Aldrin spoke as his eyes were scanning the way ahead. Both of them heard what sounded like small stones bouncing down a rock face. Aldrin pointed.

Wanda caught sight of a man ducking between two low trees. Aldrin spoke softly into a radio, which was pinned to his lapel.

"Stay here, Wanda," Aldrin directed. "We don't know where the other man is, be ready if he comes back this way."

Wanda nodded; squashing her unworthy thought that Aldrin thought she was a weak female. She moved into cover, but still had a view of Aldrin creeping up the hill. He suddenly erupted into a man-sized whirlwind, and when he stood up he was holding a struggling figure. The man shouted something in Russian, it sounded like a warning. Wanda watched for the second man, and then sensed that David and the guard had caught him.

Closely following the first scuffle, Wanda had sensed the woman again. She had to be close to have heard it – or had the man's voice carried further?

"Where are you?" Wanda thought at the hidden woman. She repeated the thought in careful Russian. A spurt of fear, and then nothing.

Aldrin and David walked back to where Wanda was waiting. The guards had the two men controlled, and were speaking to the drivers of the cars, via radio.

"Still no sign of the Russian girl and her father," Aldrin admitted. "I think those two men had lost the trail too. Are you still sure they are around here?"

"Yes," Wanda said flatly.

"Can you find them," David asked. Wanda took her gaze off Aldrin and looked away. She shook her head.

"I think I spooked her," Wanda admitted. "What is her name?"

"Tanya," David supplied. "Do you think she would come out if we called?"

"You can try, but I don't think so. If we call in Russian, she will think we are those men, and if we use American, she probably won't understand us." Wanda guessed. "But I am sure – positive – that they are close by."

After calling for more than ten minutes, Aldrin gave up. He pulled out a hand held GPS and took a reading. "We need to get back down. We'll come back again at first light with more searchers."

Wanda wanted to disagree, but there was nothing she could do and they were not prepared to stay out overnight. She obediently trotted back down the hill after Aldrin, letting David bring up the rear. When they reached the main trail, they were not far from one of the cars.

Chapter 3

The car with the two prisoners drove onto the section of the base where the detention facilities were. The other car, with Wanda, David and Colonel Aldrin, drove to the main administration block.

It was clear that Aldrin already knew his way around the base. He led the way to a small conference room. Four men sat around a table, waiting. Wanda recognised General Addison and Jim Phillips. The other two men, looked important – based on their quality suits, but were unfamiliar. She could only see them from side on.

Aldrin took a seat at the table, and was greeted as "Stev" by one of the strangers. The same man asked for a report of the search.

Wanda and David were content to stand back by the door and let the Colonel do the talking. Both Jim Phillips and General Addison glanced their way, but made no comment.

Once Aldrin had finished talking, and he had not mentioned Wanda's hunches, only the facts of what they had done, the other men talked quietly amongst themselves. None had to state the urgency to find the two Russian defectors.

"Has the plane been found?" Aldrin asked, during a lull in the discussion.

"Yes, Stev," one of the strangers assured him. "About ten miles from here. The pilot did a damn good job of getting it down. It's a wreck, but it didn't explode. The pilot and Bob Preston are both alive. Bob says the plane's instruments went out."

Aldrin nodded. "We'll be ready to go out again at first light."

The phone on the table next to Addison rang, and the General answered it. He listened, grunted an affirmative and hung up.

"Security is ready for us," he stated as he rose from his seat.

Aldrin, followed Addison and the two strangers; Jim came over to Wanda and David.

"Get some rest," he suggested.

Wanda stared after the retreating men. "Jim, I want to hear what the men say. I might pick up something."

Jim sighed. "I guess the worst they can do is tell you to leave. Come on then."

They caught up to the other men before they reached the security compound and were not challenged. Wanda and David slipped into the observation room and again kept by the door, behind all the observers. The wall opposite the door was a one-way mirror showing a room where the prisoners were being questioned.

Well, the questioner was patiently asking questions, and the prisoners were saying nothing. Wanda lost interest in the men, since she wasn't sensing anything from them. When the younger of the two prisoners suddenly spoke in fluent Russian, her mind slowly translated it. His accompanying gestures confirmed Wanda's translation of some highly derogatory and crude comments.

"Get an interpreter in there," one of the strangers commanded. It wasn't the one that called Aldrin, 'Stev'.

Aldrin, however, straightened up from where he had been leaning against a side wall, turned and spotted Wanda and David.

"Do you need to be here?" he asked, causing the two strangers to turn around.

"Who are they, Stev?" the man that knew him asked.

"Magnus, these are David and Wanda Martin. Mrs Martin spotted those two gentlemen watching this place." He added for their benefit, "Magnus Goldman, Director of the OSI."

"Commendable work," Goldman commented. "I don't think you can help much here."

Wanda shrugged, and David said, "I expect not, Sir."

They turned to leave, but Wanda paused in the doorway, looking thoughtful.

"You don't really need an interpreter. They can understand everything you are asking. They just don't want to answer. They probably speak American as well as any of us. They are putting one on you."

"And how do you know that, Mrs Martin?" the man who had so far not spoken, asked. He had risen and was now watching her intently.

"He swore in American earlier, before yelling a warning in Russian," Wanda calmly informed her questioner. "Also, that little outburst just then was mostly rude, but he told his friend there to stall for time, that the others would find the traitors."

"Is that all?" Goldman asked.

Wanda considered her answer to that. "I think they know roughly where the people are."

"Why are you so sure that they are in this area? The plane went down ten miles from here," Goldman demanded sharply.

"A strong hunch," Wanda answered at once. "Those men were watching here, but not all the time. I think they were waiting for something."

"I'm willing to back that hunch," Jim spoke quietly. Goldman glanced from Wanda to Jim and back.

"All the same," Goldman considered. "I don't think you need to be involved any further."

"They are already involved, Goldman," the important personage spoke. His tone told Wanda that his position was above that of the Director of the OSI. "And have been very useful so far."

The man was silent for a while, seeming to be considering something. He seemed to be staring at Wanda, who simply stood a bit straighter and returned his stare.

"My department has run security checks on both of them. I have been considering the reports. Provisionally, they are cleared to level six."

Wanda felt her mouth drop open, but quickly snapped it shut. Her reaction was noted by the important personage, with a very faint smile. David was equally surprised, but managed a polite, "Thank you, Sir."

Wanda added, "Yes, thank you. I didn't think anyone would trust me that much. I know that your assistant doesn't like me."

The personage did smile more then at her candid admission. "I prefer to make up my own mind, Mrs Martin. I have heard nothing but positive things from those that know you best."

Wanda decided it was wise to shut up and say no more.

Jim caught her eye and also grinned.

Wanda took David's hand and agreed to leave with him.

Chapter 4

"I'll back your hunch, Wanda," Jim confirmed his earlier statement. He had waited to speak until after he had closed the door behind him. "Let's go back to your place and you can tell me what you are basing it on."

Once Wanda had settled back into her chair and David had organised coffee for them all, Jim prompted her to talk.

She started by telling him what she had told David about her morning, followed by the row with Matheson.

"I hadn't had a chance to say anything," David confirmed, "though it was on my mind."

"Things just fell into place, Jim," Wanda admitted. "You didn't tell me much about your last mission, like who or where or why, but you did have me organising things, so I guessed a lot from how. You know what I am like – sometimes I just know things I shouldn't. So I know you got Stefan Krinsky and his daughter into the country. And David told me later about the plane disappearing." Wanda paused and Jim nodded slightly.

"OK," Wanda went on. "That girl has been broadcasting fear and pain and hunger…I've heard it here." Wanda rubbed her head, and Jim nodded again. "I have had a foul headache most of the day, and I think…I'm probably getting that from her too. David pointed out that it was like the way I react when Elisabeth is in trouble."

"But you couldn't find her," Jim noted.

"No, she shut up on me – I think I spooked her," Wanda admitted.

"She sensed you in her mind?" Jim asked, interested.

"I don't know, Jim, really," Wanda told him. "Colonel Aldrin took a GPS reading where we were, and I really believe they were not very far from there."

"Do you think you can find her?" Jim asked.

"If she starts broadcasting again," Wanda specified. "Pretty much, yes. But we have to wait until morning to go back. I am assuming they will let us go again."

"That's also assuming they stay put during the night," David suggested.

"That might be the smartest thing to do, like you told Colonel Aldrin, but if they are hungry…"

"She might try to get to the town," Wanda said suddenly. "You can see it from up there. It may not look as far away as it actually is. Though I don't know that I would want to try it in the dark."

"You wouldn't think twice if you were desperate," David pointed out. "We could wait for her at the edge of town."

"If you are right, David Martin, and if you can think of a way they will let me out of here!" Wanda argued.

"I'll speak to the Secretary," Jim stated. "I don't think that there is any more reason for that restriction. Get ready what you think you will need and I'll have David authorised to take one of the cars."

"Ah! I thought I should know that man – that was John Rossiter, the Secretary of State wasn't it?" David blurted out.

Jim nodded, "Along with Magnus Goldman, of the Office of Scientific Intelligence. So I guess you don't need telling how imperative it is to find the Krinskys."

"No, Jim. You don't. I had the message before I knew who they were," Wanda told him.

"Oh, and get something to eat before you go!" Jim ordered.

They were just finishing a meal prepared from the odd things they kept in the cottage, when there was a knock on the door. Half expecting it to be Jim coming back, Wanda answered it, only to be surprised to recognise Magnus Goldman and Colonel Aldrin.

"Mr Goldman, Colonel Aldrin. Come in – won't you. We were just about to have coffee – would you like some?"

They both declined.

"We don't plan to stay long," Goldman told her as she led them into the small lounge room. David came in when he heard the unexpected voices.

"I just came to tell you that I have put Colonel Aldrin in charge of finding Professor Krinsky and his daughter. For the time being, you are assigned to me. And I want you to assist him. Jim Phillips tells me you have a unique insight in this matter."

Wanda shrugged and didn't explain, but Goldman didn't press the matter. "Until the Krinsky's are found, you will report to me. Professor Krinsky has a lot of information that is important to us, and he must be found quickly. His former countrymen may want to kill him so he can't talk to us."

"We'll find them," David assured Goldman.

"One other thing, Mrs Martin, the movement restrictions have been lifted," Goldman added.

"Thank you for letting me know, Sir," Wanda said sincerely.

Goldman nodded and took himself off. Aldrin took a phone from his pocket and tossed it at David. "In case you need to call me," he told him.

"What if David and I are separated," Wanda asked, half teasing. "I mean, I know we are still newly weds, but we aren't exactly joined at the hip. We can't work effectively like that. What's your number Colonel?"

"Stev," Aldrin corrected her. He told her the number of his phone and the one he gave David and grinned when Wanda repeated the numbers correctly.

"Eidetic memory," Wanda muttered. "Has its uses."

Aldrin let that comment pass. "Jim says you have an idea the girl might come to the town…"

"Just a thought," David said.

"No, it's a good one, though it would take her a couple of hours to walk it," Aldrin estimated. He was thoughtful. "I will have the main road and some of the more used minor roads watched. Why don't you try to sleep for bit and I will pick you up in an hour?"

"Fine," Wanda agreed, though she doubted that she would sleep.

Aldrin left and Wanda sat down and drank the coffee David had made before their guests had arrived.

Chapter 5

Wanda didn't sleep. She knew herself well enough to know that would make her mind fuzzy and she needed it to be clear. She was once used to being awake well into the night. So, she compromised by relaxing back into the chair and concentrating on relaxing every muscle in her body.

Well, she tried that but her concentration was disturbed by wondering how it was that her mind had been able to see and feel what the stranger was thinking and feeling. She'd always been able to do this with her sister, Elisabeth, but never anyone else. Oh, she'd get hints and flashes from David, but never as clear as what she had got from this foreign stranger.

Thinking that way, made her try what she often did with her sister. She cleared her mind and thought of the stranger. She hadn't a really clear mental picture of her, just the description David had given her. Nothing.

David had also called the girl 'baggage'. She guessed that he was being polite, and the girl had an 'attitude'. Some people had once said that of her. The thought made Wanda smile, and she pondered what she would be doing in the girl's position.

After a while, she felt she was almost dreaming, or day dreaming in the sense that she seemed to be providing scenarios and having an imaginary self acting them out. But then, she felt what could only be a surge of fear, and it wasn't from herself. It wasn't her danger sense that had just kicked in. Her imaginary mind scene had been having the girl suddenly come upon a car on the road, and a very rough looking man leaning against it, smoking.

Her mind had instantly told her to hide. To keep out of sight, very quiet, off the road. Something told her mind that she had to pass that car, to get to the town. She had to get to town and back before morning. Had to. She was going to risk it.

Wanda kept thinking – more as a feeling – that going near the man was a very bad idea. She sensed that fear in the girl, and that the girl was not moving.

If only she could figure out what road it was. It was dirt, not surfaced. There were many such 'roads' up in the mountains.

"David?" she spoke softly, but her husband was instantly alert. "She's moving, but has to pass some guy by a car. I have a bad feeling, and so far she's kept back – but she really feels she has to get to that town and back by morning."

David didn't question her, simply rang Aldrin's phone. It was answered quickly, and he passed on what Wanda had said. After listening for a few moments he hung up.

"He will contact the people watching the roads, and be over shortly."

"I want to get going," Wanda told him. "I'm worried about that girl."

"She's as old as we are," David said curtly. "And if you'd met her, you'd know she can take care of herself. She just about queered that mission. We only just managed to get her and her father away. Do you realise that she was running a gang of criminals and three of her 'boys' tried to stop us taking her."

"Reminds me of me," Wanda remarked quietly. "But now – she is out of her territory, in a place where the language is strange, either she or her father is hurt, and she knows that Russians are trying to find her and possibly take them back and imprison them and possibly kill them like her mother. She won't know who to trust. Would she recognise you?"

"Perhaps," David considered. "I could show her where she raked me."

"Where's that?" Wanda asked. "You never mentioned you were injured."

David snorted. "A scratch, that's all."

Aldrin knocked at the door about five minutes later. He had a car outside, engine running.

"Any word?" Wanda asked.

"No, but there is a potentially dangerous man loose in the area. The police are looking for him. However did you know about him? It hasn't been on the radio or TV. What David told me is more specific than just a hunch." Aldrin watched Wanda's face as he asked the question.

"I can't explain it, Stev, but I often get hunches like this – usually only related to what I am doing. Actually, it saved my bacon quite often. And I can usually get a sense of what my sister is doing. But she and I are like twins. I don't understand this – I have never met this woman."

"Your friend Jim says to trust your hunches," Aldrin admitted. "My boss is sceptical, but…we'll see."

Aldrin's phone rang. His comments were uninformative. He didn't discuss the call.

When they were all in the car, Aldrin began to drive towards Wetherby, the nearest town. Wanda sat back in the rear seat and relaxed her mind, trying to sense the Russian girl again. Distracting her slightly was the police scanner that Aldrin had managed to acquire. It was apparent that her 'hunch' combined with knowledge of a dangerous man loose in the area - were being acted on. Police were searching the lesser used tracks.

Wanda hoped that she would sense when either the police came near the girl or the man decided to move. Right then, she wasn't getting anything – not even the sense of fear she had received earlier. She said as much to her companions.

Aldrin seemed unworried. "If you were in her position what would you be doing?"

"Waiting, pretending I wasn't there, wishing the guy would go and hoping he wouldn't find me," Wanda said at once. She had been in similar positions many times.

"Well, either all her mental emanations are being directed at that man, or she is no longer so afraid, so you aren't sensing anything." Aldrin suggested.

"Huh," was Wanda's comment, as she thought on that. "So what if this is a wild goose chase?"

"Do you think it is?" Aldrin countered.

"No," Wanda admitted, "But this isn't like most of my hunches."

"It is you know," David disagreed. "Like the ones you have about your sister."

"But I don't know this person!" was Wanda's argument. "And I'm only guessing that she might try for the town."

"We'll see," Aldrin repeated his earlier statement.

It took only twenty minutes to drive to the town, and Aldrin drove slowly around to familiarise himself with the place. David and Wanda were doing the same. Each considering what a stranger in a strange town would do.

"Drop me in that park," Wanda suggested. "You two can continue to drive around if you want."

"I'll walk around," David decided.

"I'll park on the eastern edge of town and look out for the woman." Aldrin chose.

Wanda was dropped off first. The park was as good a place as any for the woman to come and observe any place she might choose to visit. It was close to the supermarket and a number of other shops.

The night was mild and clear, and the moon was providing enough light to see where she was walking. The park also had occasional lights along the paths. Wanda scouted around and then chose a spot that was in shadow, but with a view to the main street, to wait.

About an hour later, David found her and crouched beside her.

"The police found that man," he whispered. "Unconscious near his car. He had some pink and yellow hair in his fist. They took him into custody, and when they went back for the car – it was gone."

"Do you think the girl took it?" Wanda asked for confirmation.

"Stev thinks it possible, so look out for a dark green sedan," David warned. "He's driving around looking for it, but she might park it out of town and walk in."

David took himself off again.

Wanda began to sense that someone was around. Not David or Stev. Her danger sense hadn't kicked in, so she stood up, keeping in the shadow, and looked around.

"Tanya?" Wanda whispered the girl's name, as well as thinking it. She sensed a start of alarm. And then her danger sense kicked in, but before she could locate the danger, something struck her head and after a moment of pain, she blacked out.

She roused, vaguely aware that someone was searching her, taking the small shoulder bag she was using. Then she felt a gentle hand touching her neck and the sore spot on her head. She blacked out again.

She became fully conscious as David gently patted her face.

"What happened?" he asked when he saw her eyes open.

"Someone hit me," she told him, using her own fingers to check her painful aching head.

"Tanya?" David asked.

Wanda tried to recall. "I think so. I think she took my bag."

"It's gone," David confirmed. "It means she will have your id."

Wanda grimaced. Her new state department id was less than a week old. "They" wouldn't be happy that she had lost it.

Alarm bells began ringing, and causing pain to lance through her head. In spite of that, Wanda began to trot towards the source of the noise.

"I'll go," David told her. "Wait here."

She didn't, but she let David race ahead and followed more slowly.

The alarm light that was flashing was outside the delicatessen, not the supermarket. There was no sign of David at the front, or of forced entry. Wanda guessed David had raced to the rear, and did likewise. She was in time to see a figure racing away and David flat out after it. She heard a police siren coming closer, and moved in that direction.

A car screeched to a halt beside her, and she turned to see the police car. One of the officers jumped out and went to the shop, the other walked around to her.

"What are you doing here?" he asked sharply.

"I was looking for someone," Wanda told him. "I heard the alarm and came over."

"Can we see some id, Miss?" she was asked.

Wanda sighed. "No, it was stolen from me along with my bag." She guessed what was coming. With well-hidden amusement, she obeyed the instruction to lean her hands on the car and spread her legs. They frisked her efficiently, and asked her to remain by the car.

The officer's partner returned to report that the shop door was forced and it looked like some food had been grabbed. A small pile of coins had been left by the till.

Wanda was aware that David had the girl as an unwilling prisoner. She waited until Aldrin had picked him up before volunteering more information.

"I was looking for a girl," Wanda offered. "She gave me a bump on the head, and I lost her. I saw some one running down the street, but I am in no condition to run anywhere."

She casually touched her sore head and brought some blood away on her fingers.

"If you need someone to vouch for me, call … and ask for Colonel Aldrin."

The mention of a military title seemed to relax their suspicions. One of the officers leant into the car and spoke on his radio, the other asked, "Will you want to be making charges?"

Wanda shook her head and wished she hadn't. "No. I should have been more careful. This will teach me."

A few minutes later, Wanda spotted Aldrin's car approaching. There was no sign of anyone else with him. She wondered where he had stashed David and the girl.

Aldrin very quickly identified himself, vouched for Wanda and had her in his car before the police recognised him. Seemed he was some kind of celebrity. He had to fend off questions, saying only that they were looking for two foreigners who had been abducted, but were believed to now be on foot in the area. The police were aware of the missing foreigners and assured him they would be watching for them too. Aldrin gave a brief description of each, and asked to be informed if either were found.

Wanda waited until they were out of sight of the police before speaking. "They thought they had their thief, nice and neat," Wanda said, amusement in her voice. "Such a pity to disappoint them, and amusing when I think that the times I was guilty I was never caught and now when I am not - I was."

Aldrin glanced at her, surprised.

"Didn't your boss warn you what a nasty piece of work I was," she said to Aldrin, watching for his reaction.

"He didn't say a great deal," Aldrin admitted.

"Well, that Tanya bird is going to get a piece of my mind when I see her. Where is she?"

"David had her," Aldrin assured Wanda. "We'll pick them up on the way back to the base."

Chapter 6

David opened the door of the motel room when Wanda knocked. She and Stev entered quickly. Wanda spotted a new scratch on David's face. She grinned.

"Have some woman trouble," Wanda chided cheekily. David growled.

"You go talk to her," he suggested. "She's in the other room."

Wanda acted on his suggestion. She saw the Russian girl tied to the bed, but glaring at her. The girl looked a mess.

"If you promise to listen, and not run off, I'll undo you," Wanda said in Russian. "We are friends, and we will help you and your father. If you want a sign of faith, I got rid of those two men who were looking for you yesterday."

Tanya Krinsky continued to glare at her.

"Well?" Wanda prompted.

Finally, she got a reluctant agreement. Wanda took it to mean that she would escape as soon as she could.

"I know that your Dad is hurt and you want to get back to him," Wanda added as she began to untie David's knots. "I know roughly where you were, we can get you back quickly and have doctors to help him right away."

Wanda knew the girl was going to struggle free when she could. In her mind she said, fiercely, "Don't you dare! And if you give me another headache, I'll give you one!"

Tanya turned pale. "Who are you?" she asked in a Russian-something patois.

"I am a friend. My name is Wanda. David, with the scratches, was one of the people who helped get you here." Wanda spoke in American, but sent her meaning mentally.

David watched from the door, and saw the two women from side on. He was struck by the resemblance in their face structure.

"Do you know the two of you could pass for twins?" he said casually.

Wanda tensed and looked more closely at the other woman. If she ignored the lurid hair colour and the shaggy dog look in was currently in, and removed the make up…

"How the hell could that be?" Wanda swore, glancing at David. He shrugged.

"What?" Tanya decided to ask.

Wanda told her, then took her wrist and dragged her into the unit's small bathroom.

"Take the make up off," Wanda suggested in Russian. "David says we could pass for twins. If you do that, and we can hide your hair, you will be less recognisable."

The other woman seemed to see the sense in that.

While she was washing her face, Wanda told her, "The police are looking for you because of that little break in you did. Lots of people, good and bad, are looking for you and your dad, because of the plane crash. Will you trust us?"

Wanda sensed that the other still didn't, and was using the motions of washing to plan her next moves. Wanda sighed.

"If you damn well want to go off and do everything by your self," Wanda told her, "We won't stop you and I damned well won't try to help you again. But my boss didn't help you escape from Russia, just to let them get you back."

"You will let me go?" Tanya asked.

David appeared behind them. He could understand Russian, but not speak it. "What will it take to get her to trust us?"

Wanda asked Tanya.

"I don't trust people who abduct me and tie me up."

"Fine, she can go. Let the police arrest her and lock her up. Then we can help her father, who is at least grateful for being out of Russia." David sounded exasperated.

"Well, if it comes to that," Wanda answered that comment by telling Tanya, "Why the hell am I bothering with someone who bashed me on the head without provocation? I am deliberately not mentioning that creep you knocked out up on the road, because that was a public service."

Tanya went pale again. "How did you know about that?" She slipped from Russian back to the mixed dialect.

"The same way I knew about those men that were after you, which is how I knew you were around. I saw a picture of what you saw, in my head. That man gave me the creeps, so I tried to tell you to hide and not let him see you. What happened?"

"He saw me when he wanted to … make water."

Wanda saw the rest of the incident in her head. Tanya had been lucky, and just skilled enough to overcome the man.

Tanya turned to Wanda, "I felt you warning me. How can you do that?"

Wanda shrugged.

David commented again, "Look in the mirror." He enjoyed the identical looks of amazement. He chuckled at Wanda's stare and added, "I thought one of you was bad enough."

Suddenly Tanya's distrust evaporated. She flung her arms around Wanda.

"Please, help my father, He's hurt, badly and I have to get back to him."

"Come and talk to Stev Aldrin," Wanda urged.

Chapter 7

Aldrin was relieved that Tanya had decided to trust them. He asked, and Wanda translated, a request to describe where her father was.

Wanda also translated the replies, even though Tanya often slipped from pure Russian to the mixture.

"He is in a kind of cave. There isn't much room inside but it is shelter and not likely to be found. It's on a rocky part of the hill, with only a few trees and bushes. The opening is very narrow, and hidden by one of the trees. Just to one side is a pile of three rocks, with paint on them."

Wanda had a vivid mental picture. "I know where to go," she told Stev and to David she said, "Can you get her back to the base? I'll go with Stev."

Tanya looked like she wanted to object when she was told she would be going with David, but she was tired and emotionally drained and agreed with reluctance.

David had a brief word with Wanda before he left. "I should take you back too, that knock on the head wasn't trivial."

"I can last out. The headache is annoying, but I will be OK," she insisted. "Besides, if I go, finding the place will be easier. I have a picture of the place, not just the description."

"Then, take this with you," David said as he pressed something metallic into her hand, deliberately keeping the gun out of sight. "You don't have to use it, but Krinsky must be kept alive, and out of the hands of his former countrymen. And I don't think there were just two of them. Oh, and your stuff is back in the other room."

Wanda nodded. She would do what she had to do.

Stev Aldrin drove as close to their earlier position as he could, before parking the car. Wanda checked her stuff and set off after him. There was still a reasonable amount of moonlight, but even so, Wanda realised that Stev's night sight was remarkable. He seemed to have no doubt of they way they had come earlier. They arrived at the GPS reference and Stev turned to her.

"Where now?"

Wanda looked around and allowed her mind to recall minor details of the pictures she'd seem in Tanya's mind. "That way." Wanda pointed up hill and slightly to the right.

Stev nodded and set off, stopping every so often to confirm that they were still going the right way. Finally they came to a place more open that they trail so far. Wanda saw the picture in her mind and pointed to the group of boulders. She was about to move up when, Stev grabbed her shoulder.

"Wait."

He seemed to scan the area very carefully. Then he nodded, and allowed Wanda to lead the way. She found the opening in the rock face and sidled in. Stev would have barely enough room to squeeze in.

Wanda was aware that Krinsky was watching her. She stopped just in the opening and spoke quietly.

"Professor Krinsky? I am a friend of your daughter. My name is Wanda Martin. I am also a friend of David, one of the people who helped you get here. I am here to help you."

A torch beam blinded her.

The Russian spoke his own language. "Being a friend of my daughter is not a recommendation I would accept. Give me a good reason not to shoot you."

Wanda laughed quietly. "Because you haven't got a gun. You and Tanya are into throwing rocks. Besides, I have Colonel Aldrin with me. Did you meet him before your plane took off?"

Krinsky dropped the rock he had grabbed up. "Yes. Where is he?"

"Stev?" Wanda called softly. She heard Stev Aldrin walk up behind her.

"Watch from the opening," he whispered.

Wanda suddenly had her danger sense kick in. She did as Stev asked, and kept in the shadow of the rocks. As her eyes scanned the area, and particularly the edge of the nearest trees, she listened to Stev and the professor talking. Krinsky had a smattering of American. He was asking Stev for his official identification.

After a few minutes of quiet conversation, Aldrin ghosted back to Wanda.

"The leg looks bad; we need to get him back as soon as we can. Have you spotted anything?"

"No, but if you ask me, someone is out there. Every thief's instinct I have is telling me to stay put." Wanda told him flatly. "What were you planning? Walking out?"

"I was, but I don't like the look of the leg. It's walk, or wait for a rescue team to get in, but we'd have to wait until first light."

"You watch for a bit. I've got an aid kit. I'll look at the leg."

Wanda changed places with Aldrin, and went to where the torch was now shining towards a wall. Krinsky was trying to stand. Wanda gestured for him to sit and she looked at the wounded leg. She agreed with Aldrin's comment.

"I'm going to bind up this wound," Wanda told Krinsky in his own language. "Keep still."

Wanda worked quickly, cutting the fabric from around the wound, cleaning it and putting a sterile dressing on it. She finally bound it to hold the dressing in place. As she worked, Krinsky was studying her face.

"Is it deliberate that you look like my daughter?" he asked finally.

"No, that was a surprise. David noticed it after we'd convinced Tanya to remove the raccoon makeup. If you ignore the hair, he reckons we could be taken for twins."

Krinsky gently grasped Wanda's face and turned it so he could see it better.

"Why can't my Tanya be like you?" he asked softly.

"Give her time," Wanda suggested. "She cares a lot for you. It took quite a few years to civilise me, and my father and I were not on speaking terms for a very long time. You're luckier."

"Thank you," Krinsky said as Wanda finished her bandaging.

"Can you try to stand on that leg," Wanda asked.

Krinsky was able to stand, if he used the wall to support him, walking, or running would be beyond him.

"Wait here," Wanda told him, and she turned off the torch.

Wanda reported softly to Aldrin.

"I tried the phone," Aldrin told her when she'd given him her diagnosis. "No signal from here. We would have to go down hill if we wanted to call reinforcements. And you were right; I have confirmed the presence of at least three men. I am sure they have this place spotted."

"Options?" Wanda asked Aldrin. He was technically in charge. She had ideas though.

"A diversion. Throw some rocks to the left and go right. I can carry the professor, there isn't much of him."

"Might work, how far can you chuck rocks?" Wanda asked.

"Far enough, I think," Aldrin said and Wanda sensed faint amusement, and the belief that he could throw a long way.

"Ok, then I will follow after a bit to watch your back," Wanda told him.

Wanda found a number of fist sized rocks in the cave, and passed them to Stev. He edged out to where he could throw and he sent them flying. Wanda heard them land some distance away. The second and third throws made it seem like they had gone that way and were slipping on rocks.

"Two of them have gone off," Aldrin said with satisfaction.

"There is at least one still watching," Wanda warned him. "What say I lead them the other way? Then you can slip out. I'll meet you at the car, but if you get there first, go without me. I'll find my way back."

"I'd rather not split up," Aldrin told her.

"I know, but Krinsky is the important one, and believe me, Stev, I have had a lot of practice sneaking away from places and losing followers."

They agreed, and Wanda sneaked out of the cave, without the man spotting her, and moved to the far side of him. She made enough noise to get his attention, but then made sure she was no more that a wraith for him to follow.

Aldrin lifted the Russian scientist into a fireman's hold as soon as they were both outside the cave. He had spotted the last watcher heading off after Wanda. He wasted no time, trotting towards the road and where he had parked his car. His speed would have astonished Wanda if she had seen him. There was no doubt in his mind that he would reach the car before Wanda, but she had been sure of her skill and he had to trust her gauge of her abilities.

He settled Krinsky in the car, made a call to bring reinforcements now that his phone had signal again, and drove off.

Wanda knew she was being followed, but she wasn't making it easy for her follower. She didn't follow the tracks, but aimed to cut directly towards Rockwater. That meant that she climbed down some fairly steep sections of the mountain. Her follower was managing to keep after her, but that suited Wanda.

The night was still; her presence was keeping any wildlife quiet. She heard a car start up and hoped it was Stev's, and she heard the sound of voices, though not the words. Some instinct told her that the original ruse had been realised. That didn't worry her. She was sure Aldrin was away, and as sure that she was able to keep ahead of the others. Her mind had a detailed mental map of the area and she knew exactly where she was going.

After about an hour, she was well down the hill and close to the areas of the mountains where visitors parked their cars to go hiking. She came to one of the car parks and saw a black SUV parked. It had a government number plate and a sticker for access to Rockwater Base. Wanda, glanced around, wondering where the driver was. She spotted the soldier, smoking a short distance away. When she started to walk over to him, she suddenly had an arm around her throat and another around her arms. Before she could struggle free, her mind went black. Her last thought was that they thought they had Tanya Krinsky.

Magnus Goldman personally greeted the Russian scientist and arranged for him to be reunited with his daughter.

David Martin brought Tanya across to the room where the Professor was waiting. In the time since she had arrived on the base and when Aldrin returned, David had provided towels, soap and fresh (borrowed from Wanda) clothes for her.

Tanya didn't exactly rush into her father's arms, but it was evident that she was relieved to see him there.

While they were talking quietly, David glanced at Aldrin. "Did Wanda come back with you?"

"No. She went off to decoy a watcher, while I carried Stefan out. She told me to go at once if I got to the car first. She was quite sure she would be alright." Aldrin noticed David seemed worried. "I notified a squad to get up there as back up."

Tanya spoke and her father translated. "My daughter shares this man's concern. She feels that something is wrong."

"Can you contact that squad, Stev?" David asked as calmly as he could.

Aldrin went to where there was a phone, and after a period of conversation, replaced the receiver.

"The squad are still on the way. There were no signs around where I had the car, and they will report when they get to the cave." Aldrin told him.

David nodded, thought for a moment, and then said, "If Wanda told you to leave without her, then she probably wasn't intending to meet you. My guess is that she would head straight back here via a direct route."

"There are some steep climbs that way," Aldrin recalled.

"That wouldn't trouble Wanda. Can you have someone check that idea?"

Aldrin nodded, and made another call. He turned back to see David studying Tanya and seeming to exchange glances. Then David stalked from the room.

Chapter 8

Wanda awoke in a very dark place, aware only of cramped and aching muscles. At first, she thought she was back in the cave where Krinsky had been. Then she rolled slightly and in the very faint light, realised that she was in some kind of room. She had been close to some kind of sofa, but on the floor. Perhaps she had rolled off it. When she tried to roll further, she realised that not only were her hands tied behind her, but her legs were bound at ankles and knees.

"Damn!" she swore mentally. It was in disgust at her position, and at the pain she was in. She moved, trying to ease the cramps and aches. Movement stirred up dust and she sneezed, making the sore muscles spasm.

She stopped moving and began a series of relaxation exercises. Some of the pain eased, and Wanda tested the bonds on her wrists, but they were too tight for her to slip out of. She rested to consider her position.

"Ok," she muttered to herself. "What do I remember?"

Her mind went back over details from when she had led the third watcher away from the cave. She had let him glimpse her, and had kept well ahead all the way down to the car park. She had heard voices at one point, and assumed that Stev's ruse with the rocks had been figured out. How soon could those others have met up with her follower? Or had her follower used a radio to call ahead?

She had got to the car park, seen the car and identified it as one from the base. She hadn't been close enough to identify the smoking soldier, before she had been grabbed. But why hadn't her danger sense warned her? Had she convinced herself she was safe? Was it because her attacker had believed her to be Tanya? They hadn't killed her. She was now assuming that her attacker was a Russian. Could there be an American working for them? Might her attackers be traitors or spies who had infiltrated Rockwater, or were there loyal guards tied up in the bushes somewhere?

Time for most of those questions later. The vital one now, was did they still think she was Tanya or did they realise their mistake?

It was a question she had no way to answer yet. She would have to play things as they came. All she could do now was find out where she was and if she could, get free.

Wanda strained to sit up, and after much struggling, succeeded in leaning her back against the sofa. Her eyes were used to the faint light, and made out shapes of other furniture draped in dust covers. The light, what little there was, came from the edges of the windows where heavy drapes didn't hug the wall. The house, in which this room existed, was no dump. She considered trying to get to the window to look out but before she could, the door opened and two heavy men walked in and came directly to her.

"No trouble!" One told her in Russian. The other cut the bindings at ankles and knees and dragged her upright. Wanda almost collapsed because her legs were asleep. The two men held her up and hustled her from the room.

Before they took her into another room, they blindfolded her and then they shoved her forward. Finally, they yanked to stop her, dragged her sideways and shoved her into a chair.

Wanda smelt cigarette smoke – or rather the smell that clung to clothes. Someone was standing in front of her.

"What do you want?" Wanda said in Russian.

Her question wasn't answered. Instead, she heard a voice say, "Get on with it."

Wanda, felt her shoulder grabbed, and before she could struggle felt a needle jab her. "David!" she screamed mentally. She thought also of Tanya and tried to send a picture of where she was, before her mind dissolved into chaos.

Her mind eventually cleared, and she once again knew who she was. Her mouth was very dry, her head ached, her eyes felt like they were full of dust and she had no tears left to wash them.

Wanda tried to recall what had happened to her, but everything was a blank. At the moment, all she knew was that she was alive, she was Wanda Martin, and she didn't know where she was or why she couldn't move.

Or was she Wanda Martin? There seemed to be someone talking to her, or calling someone called Wanda Martin and asking where she was.

Wanda moved her head, trying to locate the speaker, but the sound didn't get louder in any direction. It was just there.

"Who are you?" she tried to say but her mouth was too dry, so she thought it.

The reply made no sense. Finally, she understood, "What can you see?"

What could she see?

Slowly, her mind began to work.

It was dark. Again.

Again?

Dusty, still.

Still?

Furniture. There had been covered furniture.

Now?

Wanda forced her eyes to look. A bicycle wheel? An old wooden box? A pile of rags? Tins?

She twisted her head, but a sharp twinge in her neck forced her to move carefully. She tried to roll off her side but sharp things began to poke her in the back.

All of a sudden, a sense of danger cleared her mind completely.

"Where the hell am I?" Wanda asked herself. "Thrown in amongst junk! This looks like someone's garden shed."

The flood of adrenaline seemed to deaden the pain in her neck. She looked around, saw sunlight coming in through cracks in the boarded up window.

"Where's the door?" Wanda thought. She pushed herself up, realised that her legs were free.

The door seemed like a long way away. Between her and the door was a jumble of broken chairs, and wrecked pram, a roll of wire, on old computer monitor, and other unrecognisable things. She couldn't crawl over it.

Wanda still felt the urgent danger. She wriggled and tried to stand up. She got to her knees, but couldn't lever herself up. She looked around to see if there was something sharp around that she could use to cut the tape on her wrists. Then she identified the smell that had been getting much stronger. Smoke!

"David! David!" Wanda screamed with her mind.

"Why would they be trying to kill Tanya?" Wanda thought, as she looked again for a way out. She saw this time what looked like a trough. It was upside down, one end resting on the floor and the other on a rough wooden trestle. If the shed was going to burn, that might give her some protection. She wasted no more time on trying to get to the door or the one window. As she walked on her knees, she also grabbed some of the rags from the pile she saw.

With the smoke getting thicker, Wanda tried to call out, but her voice was too hoarse. She had no way of knocking on the walls, so she continued with her one hope and crawled under the trough and tried to make herself into a small ball. She tossed the rags into a pile in front of her and buried her nose in them.

While her mind kept yelling for David, in the vain hope he could help her, other thoughts kept intruding. Why was someone trying to kill her? They had thought she was Tanya. Did they want to kill Tanya? Or did they know that Tanya was safe and she was Wanda Martin? If they had recognised her, did they think she could tell the authorities something about her abductors?

Damn it. She didn't want to die. What else could she do? Bang on the trough. Could anyone hear that? Bang, bang. Keep trying.

Chapter 9

David received Wanda's fear sharply. He was pacing the rooms of the cottage, sure, but without proof, that something was wrong.

He tried to call Jim, but there was no answer. Wasting no more time, he ran out of the cottage and raced across to the admin building. He almost bowled Paul Matheson over.

"Where's Jim Phillips?" David demanded, without due respect for the man's position.

"Called away. Urgent Business," Matheson told him. "What's the matter?"

"Colonel Aldrin. Where is he?" David grabbed the man and almost shook him.

"With the Russians, but you can't go there!" The last was called after David who had released Matheson and raced off again.

David knew where to go, and burst into the room where the Krinsky's were being debriefed. He was aware of agitated voices in the moment before Tanya flung herself at him. She babbled in her mixed language and David had no idea what she was saying.

Stefan Krinsky spoke sharply to the others in the room to quieten them and translated what his daughter had said.

"She says Wanda is in danger. She knows this in her head. There is a dark place, full of rubbish and a fire. Lots of smoke. I don't know how she can know this."

"But where? Where is she?' David asked raggedly.

Goldman looked at the frantic David, about to insist that he left the room when Tanya suddenly spoke again.

"She says Wanda is tied up. Having trouble breathing. There are sirens." Krinsky translated.

"Where?" David demanded, but Tanya couldn't tell him.

Aldrin went to the phone and made a call. When he ended it, he went and took David's arm. "Come on. The only fire units attending calls at the moment are from Palmdale. I told the dispatcher that they might have a person trapped inside. They will tell the Fire Officer and the police. Let's go."

Wanda doggedly kept banging at the trough, but the smoke was thicker and even with her nose in the rags, it was getting into her lungs and making her cough.

"David!" she kept yelling in her mind.

She could see the glow of the fire. It must be burning fiercely out of her sight. The sirens had stopped. Surely they would be dowsing the place with water. Why wasn't the fire going out? Why weren't the firemen able to hear her banging?

The firemen were having problems. They had just come from dealing with two dump bin fires, and before that there had been a car fire and a hedge fire. Their tank was empty and now they were finding that the nearest hydrant had been vandalised.

They were now running hoses to a more distant hydrant, while the fire in the storage shed was getting a better hold. The neighbour had a garden hose on it, more to stop it reaching his fence, than concern about the shed burning down. It was, he said, full of junk like the rest of the yard. He didn't care if the whole yard burnt, so long as the fire didn't spread to his place.

He stared, as the firemen in breathing gear began to run towards the shed and use axes to break down the door. Then, they moved around to the wall that hadn't caught yet and attacked that. When they went in and carried out what looked like a body, the neighbour fell shakily against his fence.

The firemen carried Wanda out to the front of the vacant house, and while one fireman was easing her to the ground, another was fetching an oxygen bottle and mask. Wanda moved and tried to sit up and cough. The fireman supported her as the mask was slipped onto her face. They saw the tape on her wrists and cut it.

Wanda groaned slightly as circulation began to return to her hands and arms.

"Don't try to move around," a gentle voice advised her. "You are safe now."

Wanda tried to ask for water, but began to cough again.

"Relax, lady. An ambulance is coming."

Police and ambulance arrived together. One officer went with the victim to the hospital; his partner questioned the fire officer.

David arrived after the ambulance had left, almost incoherent with worry. Aldrin told him to calm down, and went to speak to the uniformed authorities.

"She's been taken to Palmdale Hospital," Aldrin told David. "She wasn't badly burnt. She had crawled under a trough, and that had deflected the burning stuff that had fallen from the roof. And she had been trying to breathe through a pile of rags."

David began to relax. A shudder of relief began to shake his whole body. Aldrin helped him back into the car.

"She's a stubborn bitch," David managed to say. "I should have remembered that. I should have…"

Aldrin said nothing, simply concentrated on getting to the hospital as quickly as he could. He'd pull rank, and do what ever necessary to get to see Wanda. The fact was, he felt slightly responsible. Illogical, but he did. And there was the matter of who had done it. They needed to know that. So, he needed to question her as soon as possible, and make sure the police kept her safe. At least until they transferred her back to the base.

Wanda remained stubbornly conscious throughout the trip to the hospital. She was aware of being lifted, being put on the stretcher and into the ambulance, then the trip and being taken into the hospital and transferred onto a trolley in the emergency department. She felt the ministrations of the doctors and heard their instructions, but had no desire to do anything but stay awake. Her mind was full of the need to be alert for another attack. If someone had tried once to kill her, likely they would try again. Any strength she had needed to be hoarded – just in case.

Though when she was offered a drink, she didn't refuse, and sipped it slowly as directed. Finally, she sensed David's presence, felt his hand gripping hers and allowed herself to sleep.

David was still with her when she woke up, still receiving oxygen or an air mixture through the face mask. She was in a hospital bed.

"Good evening," David greeted her, having recovered from his state of worry. "How are you?"

"Functional," Wanda said with a faint grin. "Tomorrow I will be fine."

"I really suspect your definition of functional. Though the doctors have told me you are recovering quickly," David managed to grin. "Are you up to answering questions yet? The police are outside the door and Stev Aldrin is hovering, and blaming himself for letting you go off by yourself. I told him he had a snowball's chance in the desert of stopping you when you were convinced of your invincibility. To which he warned that Goldman would not be amused by that attitude…so I rephrased it as you know the acceptable risks and are rarely wrong."

"Except I have had occasional – miscalculations," Wanda admitted and David knew what she was referring to.

"Was this a miscalculation?" David asked.

"Perhaps," Wanda considered. "I thought I was safe, and I had no warning of danger. None."

David was thoughtful. "Will I get that policeman in? Once they have a statement, they will let you be transferred to the base."

"Go get him then," Wanda agreed.

Stev Aldrin came in with the policeman, he was present as a representative of the State Department. He sat back and listened.

Wanda kept to facts and told the policeman all she remembered. He took notes and seemed dissatisfied that Wanda could not identify anyone that had taken part in her abduction. Hearing her story, Aldrin had a lot of questions, and was unsettled by Wanda's thought that there might be some base personnel missing. His other thought was that there might be some traitors on the base.

The policeman promised to search the car park where Wanda had been abducted, and Aldrin asked to go along. His questions would wait a bit. He had contacted the base and as far as anyone was concerned, no personnel were unaccounted for. He spoke confidentially to Goldman who promised to make enquiries. The car that Wanda had identified from the base would be examined by FBI experts.

Wanda was relieved when she was transferred to the base hospital, but not pleased that it was Paul Matheson that was tending her. Goldman insisted that the senior medico looked after her. Wanda felt that being confined to bed for three days observation was two days more than necessary.

Tanya was one of her visitors. She wanted to thank Wanda for helping her father, and also after much skirting of the issue, wanting to understand how she could have received messages from Wanda.

"We have to be related – somehow," Wanda told her. "I don't know why I could receive from you, but I could. My sister and I are able to, but not so clearly. David told me that you helped pinpoint where I was – thanks – I mean it."

"You helped me," Tanya admitted. "But – I have never done anything like that before."

"Yeah, well…I don't think I want to advertise this talent – do you?" Wanda asked.

"No, but that nice Mr Goldman wants to know how we did it," Tanya said innocently.

Wanda hid her reaction, but the last thing she wanted to do was have the 'nice' Mr Goldman getting more shrinks looking in her head. He'd likely think she was in league with the Russian agents. Wanda deliberately changed the subject.

"Who did you get to cut your hair?"

"David took me to the base haircutter," she admitted, running a hand over her very short hair. You could still see the yellow and pink stripes, but when it grew and was cut again, her hair would be back to its normal colour. "My father doesn't like it this short, but he said it was better than it was. He's glad I am away from my friends in Moscow."

"And you?" Wanda asked, sensing she was not.

Tanya shrugged, not ready to talk about that.

Wanda didn't press her, but felt the need to say a few things. "Don't take this as preaching, it isn't. David told me some things he had heard about you. I suspect much of what you were doing was some kind of rebellion. I hope you don't feel the same need here. American jails are not the nicest of places."

"They wouldn't have caught me," Tanya boasted.

"That's what I thought," Wanda told her softly. "But it wasn't the police that did. It was a bigger, nastier criminal. Once I was caught, the only way free was to convince him I was dead. The only reason I am free now, is that I put him away. I am still trying to prove I have changed."

"Why do you care about me?" Tanya asked.

Wanda grinned wryly. "Because you and I are too damned alike."

Chapter 10

Wanda received an invitation to talk to Magnus Goldman, as soon as she was discharged from the infirmary. She had expected the summons, since she hadn't been told that her "assignment" to him had ended. She had asked David where Jim Phillips was, and David had only shrugged and told her he had gone off the day she'd vanished and he didn't know where. Wanda mainly wondered if Jim knew what had happened to her.

David walked with her to the office Goldman was using while he was at Rockwater. He knocked and Goldman's voice invited them to enter. He was on the phone, but gestured for them to sit. He completed his call with, "I will keep you advised, Mr Secretary."

Goldman spoke first. "I'm glad you have recovered, Mrs Martin."

"Not as much as I am, Sir," Wanda said quickly.

"Stev gave me a copy of the statement you gave the police. Very factual and precise. There is nothing in it that I would object to, and nothing that would unsettle those who tried to harm you – should they manage to see it."

Wanda smiled faintly at the praise. She knew how to be discreet, and understood need to know. She waited for Goldman to continue.

"Is there anything else you want to add?"

"Only questions and conjectures," Wanda said evenly.

"I would like to hear them," Goldman invited, leaning back to listen politely.

Wanda didn't know what Goldman would think of what she said, since much was not based on fact but her "knowing" of things. Well, he could make of it what he wanted to.

"You know that there were people up the mountain looking for Tanya and her father?" Wanda began, and Goldman nodded. "David said that they – Tanya and her father – were originally going to come here. Then at the last minute, someone in Washington decided otherwise." Goldman nodded again.

"I was thinking that might have been why there were foreigners hanging around here," Wanda went on. "I don't know how or why the plane came down near here, but it seems to me fortuitous. Anyway, they were looking for a man and a woman around here. When I got to the car park, and saw the base vehicle, I was heading to the guard I saw when I was caught. I must have thought I was safe – because I had no warning of danger. I usually do…"

David interrupted softly. "That's a fact, Sir. But she had received a stunning blow to the head a couple of hours before."

Wanda dismissed that comment. "Anyway, the last thing I thought was that they thought I was Tanya. I think the man said 'Got you' in Russian. At that hour, another woman alone, at that place would be unlikely. Also, David has pointed out that Tanya and I show an uncanny resemblance to each other. If those men were working from a picture or description, they would still think I was her. Their description may not have mentioned the garish hair colour, and if it had, it might not be apparent in the dark. And, if they had known of the resemblance, which isn't likely because no one here had seen us together, Tanya wasn't at the base very long before Stev would have got her father back … and anyway, anyone that knew me here would still be thinking that I was a kind of prisoner and not allowed out on my own."

Wanda paused to get back to her mental list of points to raise.

"Are you suggesting, Mrs Martin, that there might me infiltrators or traitors on this base?" Goldman suggested mildly.

"I'm not, really, but …" Wanda answered, but something occurred to her. "In that house, the one that I mentioned to the police, two men came for me after I woke up. One said, 'No trouble' in Russian. I think now that the man who said it might not be a fluent Russian speaker. Later, someone said, 'Get on with it' and that was in American. That person reeked of cigarette smoke – an odd kind of smell."

Goldman leaned forward, and asked, "Get on with what?"

Wanda tensed as if a memory had just returned to her. It was something she had not recalled when she had spoken to the police. "They had blindfolded me, I thought they were going to try and make me talk, I don't remember doing that but, I just remembered that someone jabbed me."

David drew in a breath and swore softly.

"Next thing I know – I'm in that shed and the place was on fire." Wanda finished.

"Why do you think they wanted to kill you?" Goldman asked, still calmly.

"I wondered why they would want to kill Tanya," Wanda admitted, "But it didn't occur to me until later that they must have realised that I wasn't her. In that case, I was a potential witness against them or simply someone who couldn't be allowed to talk."

"Do you think that they know who you are?" Goldman asked, casually.

The question sent shivers through Wanda, David sensed them.

"I don't know," Wanda admitted, though something within her was warning her. "How could they?"

"If as you are hinting, someone on this base is involved…" Goldman left the question hanging. He saw Wanda turn very pale.

"I really don't know," Wanda said hoarsely.

"We will be alert for the possibility," David said firmly, gripping Wanda's arm and giving her his support. "I will make sure we are together all the time."

"It might be better if I organised guards for you," Goldman decided.

"No!" Wanda disagreed. "If there is someone – we don't know who it is. David and I can be alert."

"You probably had concussion," Goldman reminded her.

"I'm fine now," Wanda insisted.

Goldman kept his face impassive. He gave no indication of whether he believed her or not. Instead, he took up a folder and opened it. From it, he took a selection of photographs and spread them out on the far side of the desk. Wanda leaned forward to look at them.

"Who are these?" Wanda asked.

"People of interest," Goldman answered. "Do you recognise any of them?"

Wanda studied the pictures, immediately pointing to two. "Those are the two we caught up the hill – the ones you had questioned." She glanced at Goldman, but his face betrayed nothing. She studied the rest further. "That one, and that one, I think, are the ones I saw at the house before they blindfolded me."

Goldman looked at the two she pointed to. "Any others?"

Wanda looked at the others, sure she had not seen any of them, but her eyes kept returning to one face. Goldman tapped the photograph.

"Do you know him?"

"No," Wanda said instantly. "There is just something about him that I know – it might be something that reminds me of someone else. I have a feeling about that man."

"We might just check him out," Goldman told her.

"Those people," David commented. "Who are they?"

"Associates of known or suspected foreign agents, or known agents," Goldman told him. "Have you seen any of them?"

David shook his head, "Only the two we caught. I'll watch out for others."

"What is it that you want me to do, Mr Goldman?" Wanda asked suddenly.

"What makes you ask?" Goldman asked sharply.

"Something about Tanya and me, isn't it?" Wanda blurted. She remembered what Tanya had said. "More damn shrinks."

Goldman smiled. "It was. Tanya Krinsky and yourself seem to have an odd ability. I would like both of you to work with a colleague of mine to evaluate it."

Wanda squirmed. "It's not something I can do with just anyone. And I really don't want a big fuss about it."

"No, indeed. However, would you agree that it would be a useful thing for an intelligence agent? And I would certainly not advertise it." Goldman said carefully.

"I'll think about it," Wanda told him. "But I have had enough of shrinks telling me I imagine things."

"No rush," Goldman said. "I have to return to Washington today. So you can let me know later." He collected the photos and returned them to the folder. "Thank you both for your help."

David took that as a dismissal, and Wanda was quite pleased to leave.

Stev Aldrin entered Goldman's office after the Martin's had left. He had been listening from an adjoining room.

"Are you convinced yet?" Stev asked his boss.

"Not entirely," Goldman admitted thoughtfully. "Though she did pick up on a thought I had but, I had mentioned something to Miss Krinsky about it and the two have been talking."

"There was no way Tanya could have known where Wanda was," Stev insisted. "Wanda had to have been sending to her."

Goldman waved that aside. "I will accept, for now, that Wanda Martin has some kind of extra perceptive ability. It could be a useful skill but it could also be a security risk."

"You told me that both Wanda and David have been thoroughly investigated," Stev reminded him.

"Yes, and that has shown that there have been a number of instances where

Mrs Martin has known sensitive things – without being told. Jim Phillips told me that she had 'guessed' a lot just from the arrangements that she helped him make. She didn't admit to knowing everything, but she could have known when and where the Krinsky's would arrive."

"There is no evidence that she passed that knowledge on," Stev insisted. "She's been here…"

"But not in detention. She has been able to use all the facilities without restriction." Goldman pointed out.

"If she told anyone, that would imply prior contact with foreign agents," Stev said. "No one found any indication that she was involved with foreign agents when she was working for that crime boss – or since. She hadn't the opportunity."

"We will leave that for now," Goldman told Aldrin. "The thing that concerns me is that a Russian woman and one of ours share some kind of mind link. Maybe Miss Krinsky can do what you say Mrs Martin did."

Stev shook his head, "For someone that didn't believe in ESP, you seem to be reading too much into this. The people searching for the Krinsky's couldn't have known about Wanda. She wasn't part of the team that got them out. She was here. So, she might have known what the team was doing, but that is all."

"It's my nasty suspicious mind, Stev. Jim Phillips told me about the infiltration. They met stiff resistance to Krinsky being taken. They only escaped by inches. They should have left then, but Stefan insisted that they bring out his daughter," Goldman explained. "There was a three day gap between them taking Stefan and getting the daughter. Jim had all the relevant information on her, but she could not be found. And then, although the authorities were watching her – there was little opposition to them taking her. It was the woman's friends that caused the trouble."

"Are you implying some sort of conditioning?" Stev proposed.

"That or they put some kind of tracer on her – on the assumption that she would be taken with her father. Otherwise, I would have expected them to hold her as a means to force Stefan to come back."

"It's still all conjecture," Stev argued.

"True – but – consider this. The decision to send them direct to Washington was my idea. As Mrs Martin said, they were originally meant to come here. No one in foreign places should have known that. The decision to extract Krinsky was a closely guarded secret between the secretary, myself and Jim's team. I don't doubt any of them. The preparations here were made once the team signalled success. A matter of twenty-four hours before they arrived in America. No names were mentioned here, but if there was a spy here things might have been added together."

Aldrin nodded thoughtfully and let Goldman continue.

"I had the plane organised before Jim arrived. It was meant to have taken me back. No one at this base was told of the change in plans; the only ones that knew were you and the plane crew."

"We had a helicopter standing by to bring them here," Aldrin commented. "Have you had any report about why the instruments failed?"

"Only that they can't find a fault in the system. I'm told that an EM pulse might have done it," Goldman watched for Aldrin's reaction.

"They would have had to be fairly close to aim it and the instruments failed about half an hour out. They would risk it affecting other planes too."

"It could have been someone on the plane," Goldman suggested.

"Not the crew!" Aldrin objected.

"No, they didn't know anything until the last minute, nor were they told any names. We need to examine the girl."

"What do you mean, Magnus?"

"What I said before, some kind of implant, or mental conditioning. An EM pulse could have been directed through her, or even set off by her. She might even be able to influence minds and make the pilots turn off the instruments and have done under some hypnotic compulsion."

Aldrin didn't know what to think. "If that scenario is correct, was the crash meant to kill them?"

"Who can say?" Goldman admitted. "They didn't die and there were people in this area ready to look for them. The air route from LA to Washington comes near here anyway."

"How would they be sure the Krinsky's would come this way?"

"It didn't matter," Goldman explained. "They would be found, either by the agents or by us. If we did, this is the nearest safe place to bring them."

"What's the bottom line, Magnus?"

"Stefan Krinsky will be taken to Washington. His daughter will stay here. Until we are safely in Washington, this base will be on security lockdown. There will be a full communications blackout – no signals will be able to go out except on one secure channel. A communications umbrella will be operating to detect any attempts to pass signals in or out. Disinformation will be circulated and both Wanda Martin and Tanya Krinsky will be held incommunicado during the transfer."

"I can agree to your doubts about Tanya, but not that you don't trust Wanda," Aldrin felt the need to protest.

"Stev – I can't afford to. Even if she wasn't involved in the plane crash, she might know things now. And even though Wanda Martin has the makings of an exceptional agent, both she and Tanya Krinsky have spent time in hostile hands, which they can't remember."

Aldrin nodded, understanding. "So what is going to happen?"

"Jim will be receiving instructions, and will return here after we leave. He will be testing security and trying to draw out any enemy agents. He also needs to clear his agent. He knows the procedure."

The finality in Goldman's voice told Aldrin that if Wanda wasn't cleared, she would not enjoy the outcome. He wouldn't want his mind tampered with, to be made to forget things, have memories destroyed and risk becoming a moron. Or, the alternative of being kept where she could not reveal secrets to anyone. He suspected that Wanda would rather be dead.

Chapter 11

Jim Phillips had left after listening to the interrogation of the captured Russian agents. He had considered the implications of their presence around Rockwater, and didn't like some of his conclusions. He went to Los Angeles and from there recalled some of his team and set them to checking their back trail. It was possible that they had been followed back. He waited to hear their report, and kept in touch with the progress of the search for the Krinsky's. He was relieved when Addison told him both were found. Addison himself was to return to the meeting that the plane crash had interrupted.

Jim had the report from his team. They had found no indication that they had been followed. Or that people had asked after them. He was considering other actions when he heard a knock at his apartment door.

The messenger simply handed him an envelope and departed. Jim took it back inside and opened it. The message was simply a place and a time and a key. Such a message was not unusual. It meant that he had a mission and the details would be at the designated location. There would be no connection between the person who placed the information and himself.

Jim felt the faint rush of excitement. It was tempered by the lingering questions about the last mission, but that would not interfere with his handling of this one. He had a brief thought of including Wanda Martin and trying her out. But that would depend on what he decided needed to be done.

At the address he had been given, he found a package waiting for him. Inside was a mini CD player. After checking to be sure he was alone and unlikely to be overheard, he started the player.

The voice of the liaison that gave him his instructions had been advised of his recent activities. Jim read between the words that the Secretary of State was concerned by the national security ramifications of recent events. The briefing was phrased as if he had not been involved, it covered things that he already knew and recent events from after he had spoken to Addison. He briefly thought how fortunate it was to have Wanda and David already at the base when the voice mentioned Wanda. He wasn't worried when Wanda's hunches got mentioned. They unsettled many people. The unpleasant shock came when her disappearance was mentioned, and that she had reported being 'jabbed'. He didn't need it to be spelt out that she was now considered suspect. That point was emphasised by the demonstrated fact that Tanya and Wanda seemed to have access to each other's heads.

He thought about that - neither could be the suspected mole in the base. But Tanya might be a suspect in the plane crash and an unwitting agent, and now, Wanda might have been made an unsuspecting mole at the base.

Complications, Jim thought to himself, as he watched the 5cm wide CD self destruct. And it was fascinating how Tanya Krinsky, in the pre-punk look photo, was like a twin to Wanda. That could get people thinking the two already knew each other.

Jim began to walk back to his car, the photos tucked in a pocket inside his jacket. He let all the details he had from the briefing and what he knew of the base to mix in his head. The key person was Stefan Krinsky, but it had been made clear that he was not to be put at further risk. That was why there was a lockdown in place at the base.

There would be a communications blackout too, Jim knew, but there would be a secure channel in and out. Also, as Base Commander, General Addison would still be able to get in and out. Therefore, he needed to contact the General before he returned. He would need to get in with someone to take over the role of the Professor, while the real Stefan was taken to Washington.

He mustn't underestimate the extra care he'd need to take. Wanda had an uncanny ability to read him and know what he was thinking. And her intuition was acute, almost prescient. He recalled times when – out of the blue – she would make a suggestion that was the answer to a niggling problem – or point out a serious flaw in one of his plans.

It would be almost impossible to prevent her knowing she was under suspicion. She might even have figured it out already. He would not be able to let her be too close to him. She had admitted that her 'hunches' happened when she was. If he told her the situation and what was needed, she would do as he told her. The trouble would come if she was made to act on some pre-impressed instruction. He couldn't assume that she would, or not.

Jim considered other aspects as he drove back to his apartment. When he had the basis of a plan, he called in his team – considering the talents he needed.

And he would use Wanda – she was the best he had for picking security breaches. Where she might be a liability was in relation to Stefan Krinsky. Also, if it appeared that no one suspected her – or that she had been cleared, then the mole on the base might seek her out. Then, if she had been conditioned, there was a chance of finding out how, and negating it. That would be a favourable outcome.

Still, he would make his plans well away from the base, call his team and give them their instructions before he returned incognito with a double for Stefan.

Feeling like he had a plan, Jim began making calls – to Addison, to his team, to people who had information he needed and to someone who might be able to tell if Wanda had been conditioned.

Chapter 12

"Talk to me, hon," David finally insisted. "You've hardly said anything all afternoon."

"What's there to say?" Wanda had countered. She was sitting in a chair, resting and supposedly reading, but she hadn't turned a page in the past hour.

"There's something on your mind, and its worrying you. Tell me?" David invited.

"It's nothing," Wanda told him. "I'm just tired and my mind isn't working very fast."

David studied his wife and decided that it might be true, but she had not been herself since they had finished talking to Goldman. He mentally recalled the conversation and apart from Goldman's obvious scepticism about her ESP, he hadn't said any thing that he could think might worry her.

"Do you know when Jim will be back?" Wanda asked.

"No. Matheson said he'd been called away on urgent business." David told her. "He might have a job to do."

"And he didn't want you?" Wanda commented. "No, I guess not – Goldman commandeered us, didn't he?"

"True. And we were involved in something else," David agreed.

Wanda slumped in the chair. "I could use a good workout," she told David. "Or even a basic one."

"I'd take it easy for a bit," David advised. "You may have had concussion."

"Matheson didn't think so," Wanda spoke as if she doubted his medical skills.

"He told you to take it easy," David reminded her.

"He made me take it easy for three days! I can't afford to any longer. You know that Dav."

"Yeah! Why don't you go and do a light workout. That's my definition, not yours."

He got the first grin from her all day. Wanda much preferred to be doing something.

"I will stick to doing two laps of the perimeter and later and some in the pool," Wanda considered, "That shouldn't be too much."

David stood up and held out his hand to help her from the chair. He was relieved that she seemed more of herself.

Wanda was half way around the base on her second lap when a cacophony of klaxons broke the stillness. She stopped at the next guard post to ask what they were for. It wasn't the fire warning or the evacuation sequence.

"That's the lock down command," she was told brusquely by the guard who had gone to high alert. "You will need to return to your residence and await instructions."

Wanda thanked him and changed direction to head directly back to the cottage.

David had the advantage of the piped message that came through speakers in the cottage. First the klaxon sequence, one he had not been told of, and then the "Security lockdown initiated. All military personnel to duty stations, all other personnel to quartes to await instructions."

The message startled and alarmed him. He went to the door of the cottage and looked out for Wanda. She wasn't in sight, even when he looked from all around the cottage. If she was over beyond the admin buildings, she would hear the message and come back. He stayed at the door waiting.

Wanda had only got to the admin building when a pair of guards jogged to meet her.

"Mrs Martin? The Base Commander needs to speak to you."

Obediently, Wanda slowed to a walk and went with them.

"What's going on?" she asked them.

"Sorry, Mam," the first said. "We haven't details, only that the base is on lockdown. We were sent to get you. The Commander needs to give you instructions."

Wanda felt a stirring of excitement. She might be needed for something important. After all, she had been given a security clearance and she wanted to be helpful.

She was quite taken aback when ushered into General Addison's office and saw Paul Matheson behind the desk. He wasn't smiling, probably not surprising if he had been dragged in to deal with a major emergency and lockdown.

"You wanted me here, Sir?" Wanda asked with out managing to sound too sarcastic.

"Yes, Mrs Martin. During this emergency, I have explicit instructions that you and Miss Krinsky are to be kept incommunicado. I will have you escorted to the detention cells – please cooperate."

"What!" Wanda blurted, stunned but sensing something was not right. Her first thought was that it was all Matheson's idea. "I was given a security clearance. This isn't fair."

"Fair isn't relevant. I have orders I must follow. Everyone on the base must cooperate or be detained," Matheson was not smiling as he explained.

"I heard the message," Wanda argued. "Non military personnel were to go to their quarters. That's were I was going. I promise to stay there."

"The message indicates to await instructions. I am giving you instructions. The detention cells are quite comfortable and I have been instructed to house you in one."

"Can I talk to David?" Wanda asked.

"No. The instructions say incommunicado. You are not permitted to communicate with anyone. I will advise your husband of these orders."

Wanda felt mutinous and this must have been clear in her expression.

"Mrs Martin, please co-operate. If you don't, I will have to sedate you. That is also in my orders, although I think that is extreme."

"Knock me out! What ever for? I am no security risk," Wanda protested.

"I believe it is because you seem to have some ESP thing that people don't understand."

Wanda felt herself go pale. "Alright, I will behave myself. You won't need to knock me out."

"Very good," Matheson told her as he gestured to the guards. He seemed to stare at one of them for a moment.

The guards weren't treating her like a dangerous person, but they were performing the duty in a professional manner.

Wanda wasn't happy. She still thought this was all Matheson's idea because he didn't like her. However, if she couldn't prove it, it would be prudent to obey him. She felt she was still only barely trusted, in spite of the clearance. If this was actually decreed by a higher authority – it wouldn't do to disobey.

Even though she had no intention of escaping, some instincts were too deep to unlearn. Wanda did a quick mental inventory. Jogging gear didn't permit much in the way of options for lock picking. She gave the detention cell an automatic scrutiny, noting all the security features.

"It'll do, I suppose," Wanda muttered.

"Mam, I have to check your pockets," the guard that spoke had 'Harris' on his uniform.

Wanda permitted the impersonal search. She was allowed to keep her handkerchief but not her iPod or watch.

"They aren't Mata Hari spy devices," she grumbled. "And I need something to do or I will go crazy."

"Mam, I will speak to the Commander. If it is checked you may be allowed to have it back."

"Thanks," Wanda acknowledged, turning to examine the room further. The two guards retreated.

Chapter 13

David strode into the office where Matheson sat and demanded, "Why is Wanda in detention?"

"Calm down, Mr Martin," Matheson said sternly. "I was acting on orders."

"Can I talk to her?" David insisted.

"No communication is allowed. Mrs Martin and Miss Krinsky are to be kept incommunicado."

"Whose stupid orders are they?" David insisted then. He was in no mood to be courteous.

Matheson kept his anger at the interruption under control.

"Mr Goldman made that requirement. When the lockdown is lifted, they will be released at once. That won't be until the threat to this base is removed. Now, I require you to return to your quarters and stay there. Our priority is to guard the Professor, and should you cause more trouble, I have the power to detain you too."

The threat cooled some of the reckless ideas in David's mind.

"May I ask if the threat was against the base or the Professor?" David asked in a more civilised tone.

"It is effectively the same thing," Matheson said. "I believe that the threat is because the man is here. We were preparing to move the Professor to Washington; however he must now remain here, as it is deemed unsafe to move him."

David nodded. That made sense, even if detaining Wanda didn't.

"Will General Addison be returning?" David asked.

"Yes, after he has been thoroughly briefed on the situation. He will however tell you exactly the same as I did."

David stared at Matheson for a moment, and as he was considering leaving, recognised Wanda's iPod on the desk.

"Is that my wife's?" he pointed.

"Yes. It has been checked for content and function and she will be allowed to have it back."

There was nothing more he could do, so he turned and stalked out. Matheson logged the incident and returned to the reports received so far from squads searching the base for explosives.

David didn't go far after leaving Matheson. After stalking out, he had slowed his pace. He was still angry that they had felt the need to put Wanda in detention, but if it was Goldman's idea, the reason wouldn't be petty spite. Perhaps it was something to do with whatever Wanda had sensed during their talk with Goldman. The thing that had got her worried and made her uncommunicative.

The sound of someone approaching, wearing combat boots or his footsteps would not have been so loud, made him decide to dodge out of sight. David tried the nearest door. It was Stradbroke's office, and fortunately unlocked and should be empty.

Looking through a fine slit in the not closed door, David saw two guards trot past and stop outside Addison's office. One knocked and entered. Moments later, Matheson emerged after the guard, looking angry. He stopped and entered his own office and re-emerged with his medical bag and followed the guards again.

When the passage was again quiet, David emerged. On an impulse, he went to Addison's office. It was locked, but that didn't stop David. He wasn't as good with locks as Wanda, but handy enough and he guessed that Matheson wouldn't have set any alarms.

Inside the office, David went directly to the desk and found what he was hoping to find – the hard copy of the lockdown orders. They did indeed contain specific orders concerning Wanda, and the Krinsky's. The Professor was to have a special guard and only specific people were to be allowed near him.

David glanced quickly through the other papers, being careful to replace things as he found them. He found a folder with Wanda's name on it and glanced inside. In it was information about her past, including her criminal record and known past activities. It was marked confidential, and David didn't think Matheson should have had need to access to it – though he probably did have the clearance. He re-hid the file exactly where it had been and decided it was time to get right away and think things over.

He was challenged once on the way back to the cottage, but allowed to proceed after claiming to have been called to see Matheson.

The first thing David tried when he got back to the cottage was to call Jim Phillips or even Stev Aldrin, who had gone off after debriefing Wanda at the hospital. The phone was dead. He tried the battery operated radio, so he might listen for the news broadcast, but all he got this time was static. He tried his computer, it had a wifi connection and he usually had no trouble logging onto the internet through the base computers. That too didn't work. Annoying, but he guessed a communications block made sense. He flopped into a chair and tried to think.

Krinsky, David thought. He was the key to everything. Aldrin had gone to arrange a helicopter to fly him out, but now, thanks to the security scare Aldrin couldn't come in and Krinsky had to stay.

The rumours he had heard ranged from a bomb scare through a range of other terrorist attacks. Whatever the truth, it was probably aimed at getting at Krinsky. He would go and talk to the man if he were allowed, but even if he did what could the man do?

What could he do himself? David had backed down because he didn't want to risk being locked up. "Surely, they can't think that Wanda could be involved in this bomb scare or Tanya either, for heaven's sake."

With out conscious thought, he moved to stand by the window where he could watch the main gate.

David didn't have to find an excuse to speak to Addison, he was sent for. The manner of the two marine guards suggested trouble. He didn't care. He had had all night to stew and fret. He had his anger under control – barely. During the night, as he maintained his vigil, watching for Addison to return, he had been aware of some sort of excitement over in the detention quadrant, and then he had seen squads of guards deployed to search the base. Things had quietened down after two hours, and had been quiet for at least that long again.

In a deep part of his mind, he knew Wanda had been involved in the fuss. Not that he had any telepathy, he didn't, but Wanda could sometimes send to him because they were so close. It was usually like emotions, not thoughts, like if she was in danger, or angry.

During the fracas, he'd sort of sensed anger, but it had seemed wrong. Not in a way he could explain, and since things had settled down, he didn't have any sense of Wanda at all. Like she was asleep. She could be, but…

"David Martin, Sir,' his marine escort announced after opening the General's door.

"Come in," was the firm invitation in Addison's familiar voice.

David went in, saw Matheson and clamped his mouth shut. He knew his dislike of Matheson was irrational, and probably due to Wanda's dislike of the man.

"Sir," David greeted Addison. "You wanted to se me?"

"Yes," Addison agreed, speaking from behind his desk. He didn't invite David to sit. "I understand you were causing trouble yesterday."

David flushed, realising that Matheson had reported him. "That wasn't my intention, Sir. I was concerned about my wife."

"So I understand. However, the instruction to place her in detention was as much for her protection as for security purposes. Goldman was concerned that the present emergency is related to the presence of Professor Krinsky. There are many other details that I am not at liberty to reveal."

David looked at his feet while he got himself under control. "Why don't you just move the Professor, and then it won't matter." He felt he had managed to sound suitably matter of fact.

Matheson spoke up. "That might be exactly what the other side want – to get him out of this secure place. Moving him could be opening him to the risk of assassination or abduction."

David counted ten. "How long then, will it take to clear this emergency up?"

"As long as necessary," Addison told him. "There have been specific threats made and we are working to confirm or dismiss them. What is your real concern, David?"

Taking a deep breath, he said, "My wife needs to keep active, Sir. In a small room, that's hardly possible. If she doesn't, she could get sick again."

"Your wife is meant to be taking it easy," Matheson said sternly. "She had a concussion, and should not even be considering any dare devil stunts for at least a fortnight."

"Wanda does those for fun, not exercise," David told him, feeling faint amusement at Matheson's shocked expression. Addison's expression was slightly less severe.

"Does she walk out of secure rooms for fun too?" Matheson demanded. "And attempt to fight marines twice her size – for fun."

"What? What are you talking about?"

Matheson explained. "Your wife, who should have been in a secure place, was observed trying to break in to the quarters given to the Professor. When challenged, she took on two marines, managed to overcome one and got away from the other. She refused to obey commands to stop."

"What did you do to her?" David demanded.

"No more than necessary," Matheson said coldly. "She was eventually restrained, but was totally out of control. She is now under sedation, as I should have done in the first place. Though at that time I considered that to be excessive. Apparently, Goldman expected this."

David opened his mouth to speak, but couldn't think of how to phrase it tactfully. Finally, "I don't believe that Wanda did this of her own will. Some one had to have made her. She had no reason to resist your orders or to go near Krinsky."

"Are you suggesting something, David?" Addison asked mildly.

"No, Sir, I am just saying that the actions are incompatible with my wife's intentions of proving she is not some kind of maverick."

Addison appeared thoughtful. "Sit down, David."

David was grateful for the chance.

"Paul, would you go and check those reports from Alpha sector," Addison instructed.

Matheson went without a word. From the corner of his eye, David saw what might have been a satisfied smirk on Matheson's face.

Addison dismissed the marine guards. When he had checked that the door was properly closed, he returned to sitting behind his desk. He was quiet for a while and then spoke gain, only this time, his voice was different.

"You are not thinking clearly, David. What is really worrying you."

David looked up sharply. The face hadn't changed just the manner.

"Jim," he whispered in disbelief. The General simply smiled.

"David, Wanda will be well enough. I was the one who suggested that she and Tanya be kept well away from everyone."

"But why?"

"I'll come to that. What do you think made Wanda get out?"

"That's just it. I don't think she would. I wasn't with her when she was picked up, but I think if the situation was explained to her, and she knew it wasn't just Matheson's spite, she wouldn't jeopardise her chance to work for you."

"How was she before the lock down?"

David's face betrayed his alarm. "Okay at first, she was glad to be rid of Matheson and out of the infirmary. After we spoke to Goldman she was sort of quiet. She denied that anything was worrying her. I thought it might have been after reaction to all she'd been through."

Jim/Addison nodded. "David, I had a number of reasons why I wanted Wanda and Tanya out of the way, sedated preferably. The main one is their apparent telepathy. I can't judge the limits of it."

"And if she was close to you, she'd know…" David felt his anger dissipating.

"Exactly. She would probably pick up things that I do not want her aware of."

"Fair enough. Obviously you have a job to do here and you probably won't tell me things in case Wanda senses them from me. It seems though that you don't trust Wanda."

Jim looked at him with compassion.

"Goldman told me that Wanda remembered being jabbed when she was a prisoner. Did you hear that?"

David nodded, feeling ill.

"Since the people involved are working against Krinsky, it must be assumed that they influenced her. They might have thought she was Tanya. They might have realised she belonged here. That might be why she tried to get at Krinsky last night. And you know – if anyone could get out of secure quarters, she could."

"But they tried to kill her," David hissed.

"We don't have the full details, David. But that changes nothing. As much as I dislike the need, I cannot trust Wanda until I have proved she hasn't been turned into an enemy. Goldman realised that as soon as Wanda mentioned the injection. We don't know what they did to her."

"But…" David realised now what had been on Wanda's mind.

"I have a plan, David," Jim said calmly. "To clear Wanda and to lure out any moles on this base and I will need your help."

Chapter 14

Wanda became aware of someone massaging her legs. She was lying on her front in an unfamiliar bed.

"David?" she tried to say. The massaging stopped and someone put a straw to her mouth.

"Drink slowly, Hon," David advised.

"What happened?" Wanda asked, rolling over and trying to sit up. Her head felt like it was rotating.

"Take things slowly for a bit," David warned her. "You've been lying down a while."

"What happened?" Wanda repeated.

"You've been out to it," David said with forced calmness.

"That SOB," Wanda muttered. "He did it! Why?"

"He had orders," David told her. "Addison confirmed it – but he let me in to massage you each day."

"He said…that if I co-operated, he wouldn't."

"Let it be, Wanda. OK?"

"I don't want to!" Wanda sounded more peevish than angry. "Is Jim back?"

"Yes, he came in this morning. The lockdown is lifted but the base is still on alert. How are you feeling?"

"Unspeakable," Wanda told him. "And a bit stiff. Am I allowed out?"

"Yes. Can you walk?"

"I can walk," Wanda said before she had even tried. She had to get moving before the stiffness became painful.

David gauged the deliberate stride and knew Wanda was forcing herself to move. With the sickness she was chronically fighting – too much rest and inactivity could be fatal.

The past week had set back her recovery. As she was now, Matheson had no need to fear her doing dare devil stunts.

Wanda reached the cottage, and needed to cling to David. She was trembling from unvoiced pain.

"Come in. I will run a hot bath," David urged his wife. Wanda found the courage to move.

They passed through their small front room without Wanda noticing Jim waiting there. David did and simply exchanged glances with him. That Wanda hadn't sensed him was proof of how much of her attention was taken up with how she felt.

David returned after helping Wanda into the bath. Jim waited for him to speak.

"It's not too bad," David finally said. "The hot bath should help."

Jim accepted David's diagnosis. "Do you think that she recalls what she did that night?"

"No. She couldn't understand why Matheson knocked her out," David said unhappily. "That's not good is it?"

Jim didn't reply directly. "It implies things though."

"What?"

"It seems to confirm that she was 'conditioned' and they either implanted a compulsion, or there is someone on the base that knows how to activate her."

"How could they be sure that Krinsky would still be here when Wanda got back? Or, how Wanda would be able to get to him?"

"They couldn't be sure," Jim agreed.

"Unless they made the threat so he'd have to stay?" David proposed.

Jim didn't tell him that the 'threat' had been a deliberate sham.

"Perhaps," Jim murmured. "I'm tending to think that they thought they had Tanya and worked on her assuming she would stay with him. I think that it was after they had done that - they realised it wasn't Tanya and decided to kill her."

"But she survived," David went on. "And someone recognised her…"

Jim nodded.

"Damn it, Jim, what are you going to do?" David's voice shook.

"Be easy, David," Jim said gently. "Let's see how things work out. Who could have spoken to Wanda after the lock down?"

"The guards that took her to Matheson at first, Matheson, the guards who caught her at night, me," David considered.

"What about before that - after she came back from the hospital?"

"Matheson had her in the infirmary. I wasn't there all the time. Anyone might have dropped in. I guess who ever it was made her forget she saw them."

"Hmm," Jim mused. "Do you know any of the guards?"

David shook his head. "I wasn't there. Ask Wanda."

Jim quizzed David for a while and then desisted.

David stood up, took Wanda's iPod from his pocket and put it on the table and went to see how his wife was.

Instead of her being relaxed, she was sitting in the water, hugging her knees, crying silently.

Ignoring the water, David knelt beside the bath and hugged his wife.

"You'll be fine," he tried to reassure her.

"Don't lie to me, David. I did something horrible, didn't I?"

"Not horrible, and Jim knows it wasn't your fault."

"What did I do?"

"Got out of the detention cell and headed for Krinsky. You didn't get there. The marines saw you."

Wanda nodded. "I don't recall that. And I didn't have anything on me to use on the lock."

David let that pass. "Jim knows it wasn't your fault," David repeated.

"That's no consolation," Wanda told him looking miserable. "It means someone has screwed with my head. I won't be able to work for Jim."

"It will be fine. Jim has a plan."

"So do the owners of a hurt puppy when they take it to the vet to be put down."

"Daft woman! Jim wouldn't hurt you. I wouldn't let anyone hurt you!"

"No, it will be someone that doesn't know me and who would only see me as a problem to be fixed."

"Get dry, dressed and come and talk to Jim," David insisted, wanting Wanda to get off that train of thought. "He certainly isn't talking about casting you asunder."

Wanda said nothing until she was almost dressed. "He can't afford to trust me. With my perfect memory, and knowing what Jim does and what the Secretary would disavow – I could be a political time bomb in the wrong hands."

"You are exaggerating!"

"Am I?" Wanda challenged. "I could go with you today and sit on a hotel balcony overlooking the sea and only be interested in it and you. Three years later, some one might come to me and say 'You were at this hotel three years ago, well on that day, vice President B was there. Did you see him?' I could think back to that day and all the details I didn't consciously note would come to mind. I could recall them and say – Oh yes, he was there he was having dinner with President A's wife."

"You aren't like that," David told her.

"No – but what if I don't know what I'm saying or doing?"

David controlled sudden nausea. "I trust Jim! Come and talk to him."

Wanda nodded and decided she needed to know the worst.

"Get coffee, Dav," Wanda suggested. She wanted a private word with Jim first.

She edged into the front room and studied Jim's profile. He seemed serious, introspective.

"I'm sorry, Jim," she said, startling her mentor. Jim looked around but didn't greet her with his usual smile.

"What for?" he asked.

"Don't play innocent. You know someone messed with my head while I was missing. I haven't even started really working for you but I know what you have to do if one of your team goes missing. You are going to have to ditch me, aren't you?"

"Not necessarily," Jim told her, and he wasn't avoiding the issue. "Yes, there's a procedure and yes I will need to send you away for a few days. I have contacts who might be able to tell if and how your mind has been conditioned."

"You know damn well it's been screwed," Wanda said bitterly.

"Do you want to keep working for me?" Jim challenged.

"You know I do!"

"Then listen," Jim urged. "Do what I ask. I still need your help. I will tell you about that later – after you get back. Though Addison wants to know how you left the base unnoticed."

Jim sensed Wanda relax.

"My associate is very good at what he does," Jim assured her. "And any one who tries to screw your mind, as you put it, won't have taken into account your talent for 'knowing things' and I trust you."

Wanda sensed this truth in his mind and something else.

"Alright, Jim, I will be the bait for your fishing expedition," Wanda agreed with the thought that had been in his mind. "Though you do realise that the bait is usually thrown to the fishes."

Jim laughed at the way she had twisted his meaning. "Get some rest. You will need to leave early. David will drive you and we can talk again when you get back."

Wanda sensed Jim's satisfaction as he called a goodnight to David. She felt herself relax.

Jim continued to chuckle at Wanda's comeback until he was back in the admin building. Far enough, he hoped, for Wanda not to read him. His associate could not give him guarantees. At least he had hidden that from her as well as many other things he still didn't want her to know. It had been hard work and he hoped David would be distracting her in another way by now.

Chapter 15

"We are being followed, Dav," Wanda told him after they had been on the road for a while. They had been travelling in silence with only the radio for distraction.

"Jim said that he would have a man following us. That is probably who you sense."

"What else did Jim tell you," Wanda asked peevishly. It was a symptom of how worried she was. In spite of Jim's reassurance.

"Not much. Do you want to stop for a drink and a rest room?"

Wanda sensed a reason and agreed. The found a fast food place and parked in their lot. When they had their drinks and were seated in a quiet corner, David continued the conversation.

"Jim simply said that as far as the base personnel that need to know are concerned – you are only going to see your specialist, Rickard." David forced a chuckle. "And the rumour mill probably will be suggesting everything from you've been taken ill through being fired or arrested."

"Misdirection. What else did Jim tell you?" Wanda stared at David as she drank her thick shake.

"Well you are to see Rickard this afternoon; he will keep you at the clinic as long as he needs for the tests he wants. You should know all that better than me."

"Yeah. What else?"

"After that – if no one seems to be taking an interest in you, we've an appointment with the North American Paranormal institute. Just to see if they can give us some measure of what you can do."

"I can't talk to ghosts," Wanda retorted quietly. "Then the shrinks, right?"

"Ye-es," David agreed. "I don't know what that involves, but Jim says you have met the bloke before."

"Where?"

"He didn't tell me, just smiled and told me it would keep you guessing."

"Damn him," Wanda said without anger. "So why couldn't you tell me this in the car?"

David groaned. "So much for Jim's advice – if I don't think about it you won't ask. It's only that he didn't have time to have the car checked for bugs before we left."

"Is he getting paranoid?"

David shrugged. "I think it is to keep people guessing. We only told Addison and Matheson about the specialist. Jim used the excuse that he didn't like the way you were looking when he saw you."

"So if someone is screwing with my head – they'll suspect other motives and try to find out," Wanda deduced. "So if I say anything it's just about Rickard – as if nothing else is going on – but giving them chances to show themselves."

"That's my clever girl," David grinned. He felt pleased that Wanda hadn't picked up on other things Jim had told him – which Wanda wasn't to know.

Wanda sighed as she walked back to the car. Of course David knew things that she wasn't allowed to know. David wasn't worried, though, so she left the matter alone.

They continued on towards the clinic, speaking only of unimportant things.

When they arrived and had parked, Wanda glanced around looking for the 'tail'. She saw a clean cut man getting out of a van who glanced their way. He took a pile of something out of the van and put it on its roof. Then he ducked his head back in for something else. This time he took out what might have been a lap top.

David told her to 'come on' and she let him lock the car doors.

"Which way?" David asked, even though Wanda knew he had been there before.

"Front way will do," Wanda told him, and allowed his hand to grip hers.

When they were away from the car, David whispered, "You were right. We were followed by someone other than Jim's man. He just gave me the signal. Don't try to work out who they are. Willie knows which car and will take care of things. He will also check over our car. Two can play this game."

Wanda smiled, sure of the expertise of Jim's people.

Once she got to the clinic's reception desk, and announced herself, she had no time to consider other things.

The staff were expecting her and they went quickly through the admission procedure. David stayed until she was settled into the private ward.

Wanda had her iPod around her neck and was about to put the ear buds in her ears when a young looking doctor entered.

"Mrs Martin," he greeted with a cheerful smile. "I'm Dr Lang. I'm here to do some preliminary tests – nothing strenuous."

"What about Dr Rickard?" Wanda asked.

"He has been delayed and won't be here until this evening, but he has asked me to get the initial blood tests done. Hopefully, the lab will have the results by the time he arrives."

"I guess you won't need me for a while," David said tactfully. He hopped off the bed and moved to the door. "I'll be back later."

Wanda waved him off, and Dr Lang began to pull the curtains around the bed. He unlocked a cupboard on the wall and began to take out what he needed for the blood samples.

Wanda, knowing the procedure rolled up her left sleeve.

As the doctor took the sample, he spoke softly. "It is quite safe to talk here when the curtains are closed," he told Wanda. "So tell me what you remember about the day you were abducted."

The question was totally unexpected.

"Are you a doctor or a shrink?" Wanda asked him.

"Both," he admitted. "I work with Jim at times."

Wanda studied him. She recalled the face – the place would come to her.

"The hot springs town. You never said a word!" Wanda guessed aloud. At the time, he had been with a disguised Jim Phillips. "So, you know what a rat bag I used to be."

Lang smiled. "What do you remember about the other day?" he reminded her.

Wanda repeated what she had told Goldman. She was watching Lang's face, but it betrayed nothing. Then, without prompting, she told him what David had said of her unrecalled night foray.

"Yes, and you took on two marines," he confirmed, and smiled at her astonishment.

"No wonder Matheson knocked me out. That was a stupid thing to do," Wanda admitted. "I'm really screwed, aren't I?"

Lang didn't answer that, instead he told her, "When you went to the hospital after the fire – they took a routine blood sample to test for drugs. Now, were you on any medication for any thing at the time?"

"No," Wanda said, sinking back on the bed. Lang had finished his blood taking and now was testing her pulse and blood pressure and heartbeat. He had her right wrist in his hand. "What did they find?"

Lang told her the long-winded chemical name, and then added, "It can be used to aid a subject to relax for hypnosis."

Wanda felt pale and shaky. "Then you had better do your worst," she told Lang with resignation.

"On the contrary, Jim told me I had better do my best," Lang told his patient, and was relieved when Wanda grinned faintly. He came and sat on the bed and held her wrist again and spoke gently.

"I want you to relax. Completely relax."

With all the worries on her mind, Wanda found that difficult, so Lang suggested images for her to think of. When he sensed her pulse rate become slower, he continued.

"Focus on a point in the middle of my forehead."

Lang watched Wanda's eyes as he continued. "Relax completely as you watch it…Good….breathe deeply, in, out, in, out … that's it…relax."

Wanda only felt as if she had dozed off for a moment, except that Lang was no longer sitting on the bed.

"Well?" Wanda demanded, as she watched Lang putting one of the tubes into a separate plastic bag.

"Oh, I'll need to talk to you again," he told her matter-of-factly. "Later today, or when you are free. We will need a few sessions."

Wanda sighed.

"So, what are you going to do until Rickard gets here?" Lang asked. "I think you should stay in this room for now."

Some instinct warned Wanda, so she asked, "How come? I thought I ought to go for a walk- get some exercise."

"Jim said you were quick on the uptake. He has a discreet watch on you. He is not expecting trouble, but this room has been prepared for you. With these curtains around, there is a damping field in here so we can't be over heard."

"Well, in that case, I will be here listening to my iPod, and pretending that I like being kept in a small room."

Lang didn't miss the bitterness in her tone, but he said nothing, only "I'll be back later."

"What did you find, Doug?" Jim Phillips asked When Doug Lang called him on a secure phone link.

"I think there is no doubt, that hypnosis has been used on her. I questioned her under hypnosis and she said things that indicate her mind was remembering a previous hypnotic session. I can't find out what trigger words or acts are implanted. She did tell me that Krinsky was a dangerous man and he had to be killed or returned to Russia."

"Damn!" Jim swore softly. He was quiet while he thought things out.

Lang waited for Jim to speak again – well aware of his friend's dilemma. His own impression of Wanda was a favourable one. She was bright, intelligent, and intuitive and from what he already knew – courageous and did not let fear paralyse her. In short, she was ideal for the work that Jim did.

"I want to use her for this mission," Jim said finally. "Is there anything you can do, so we can regain control if she is compelled by others?"

"I can't guarantee success, Jim, but we could try implanting our own commands. It would also help if we knew how they would get their commands to her."

"I will work on that. There has to be at least one person at the base. I have an idea of how to find them. Can you organise to implant a subcutaneous audio receiver/ transmitter?"

"Yes. Do you have such a thing?"

"I think Brendan can make one," Jim said, smiling grimly. "That way we can monitor her without making it obvious and perhaps pick up some trigger words."

"If we do, I could do something more," Doug said, more hopeful. "When you work it out, tell me what you want Wanda to do, or not do, and I will do what I can."

Chapter 16

Wanda was telling David about the past two days. He had been absent, but keeping in touch with her by phone. It wasn't hard to deduce that he was doing things that Jim didn't want her aware of. She tried not to be resentful.

"So, Rickard is pleased with me. The tests were all good, at least the ones he was interested in. It seems that the treatment they gave me is still working. He told me Elisabeth was doing well too."

"That's good," David agreed. He knew Wanda regretted not being able to keep in close touch with her sister. "What about the mind games?"

Wanda pulled a face, even though David wouldn't see it at the end of the phone. "Interesting," Wanda summarised the testing that the paranormal researchers were trying on her. "As far as they can tell, what I can do is intermittent. But I have definitely got something out of the ordinary."

"That tells me nothing new," David complained.

"Well, I did really well on the guess the cards game when the person knew what it was. I wasn't as good when the other person didn't look at the card. I told them that I wasn't seeing the card in my head or hearing someone tell me what it was. I just knew. I also said I knew a lot clearer when it's about something dangerous to me."

"So…" David prompted.

"So, they can't really deduce much yet – after only one day. They would like me to come to their research lab, to try more things. I said, I didn't think so. I did tell them about Elisabeth and Tanya and…mum, and they think I have something they call empathy too. That's more about sensing emotions."

"Could they improve what you have?"

"I don't really know, Dav, but do I need to? I freak enough people now and I can use what I have."

She heard David sigh and added, "Or do you really want me to read your mind, even over the phone and find out what sneaky underhanded things you are doing for Jim that I am not meant to know."

"Damn it, Hon, you can't do that can you?"

Wanda chuckled. "No, I just wanted to know if you wanted me to. You can't stop me being a good guesser. So how much longer do I have to stay here?"

"Not sure. I'll ask Jim when I speak to him. Anyway, I'll talk to you tomorrow."

Just when she was feeling totally useless, she heard the door of her room open. She glanced up, hoping it was David, but it was Jim.

Her smile faded as she sensed his concern.

"So what's the verdict?" she said with a completely flat tone.

Jim chose to sit on the visitor's chair, after closing the curtains around the bed. He seemed to be choosing his words.

"I'm not going to play this down. You have been hypnotised and there are indications that the people will try to use you against Stefan Krinsky. Doug is working to counter that."

Wanda nodded, trying to read Jim's expression.

"Now, I really need your skills for part of something I am doing. That is checking the security at the base. Addison knows you got out unseen before all this started. And you have been there long enough for your baser instincts to have studied the security…"

Wanda laughed, realising that Jim was teasing her, and she relaxed slightly.

"Yeah. It's a force of habit."

"Good, because there is going to be a meeting of the top scientists at the base. Rather than sending Stefan to Washington as originally planned."

Wanda nodded. She wasn't sensing anything from Jim at the moment. He might have been reciting from a prepared script rather than being the planner of all.

"What if someone makes me go for Krinsky again?"

Jim smiled faintly. "Stefan will be well guarded and neither you nor Tanya will be allowed near him until after the meeting. Should you try, you will be stopped."

"I hope they won't be authorised to use deadly force," Wanda said, only half joking.

"Sufficient force," Jim clarified. "In your case, the guards know you can better one and a half marines."

"Ouch," Wanda muttered. "I gather that small and innocent looking won't help me?"

"No," Jim confirmed. "However, you won't need to worry about that. I have an idea to explain to you later. I believe it will be safe enough to have you checking the security with me. The people who had you won't know of this meeting and your nefarious skills."

"You can't be sure of that," Wanda presumed.

"No, so that is why we will check that there is no way people we don't know about can get onto or off the base."

"Fair enough," Wanda agreed.

"You will still be fish bait. You will seem to have been cleared of any suspicion, but since there is a traitor on the base, once they learn what you are doing, they may try to contact you. So, having been warned, be alert for any unusual approaches."

"What if it is too quick or they make me forget?"

Jim reached for something in his pocket. It was a small box with a tiny metal object inside. Jim explained what it could do.

"We can implant it behind the earlobe and it should pick up everything you hear. David will also be keeping an eye on you."

"Clever. No one will think it odd if we work together, and I'm sure David won't mind."

"Good girl," Jim told her, seeing the gleam in her eyes. "I'll brief you when you get back. I will have David here the day after tomorrow."

There was a slight feeling of discomfort behind her earlobe where Dr Lang had implanted the tiny listening device. The procedure hadn't taken long and had only required a local anaesthetic. She was told that it was covered by a layer of synthetic skin. She resisted the urge to feel for the lump.

David was driving her back to Rockwater, four days after they had departed. Jim's man, Willie, was again tailing them, but keeping well back. Before they'd left, David had warned Wanda that there was a 'bug' in the car. He had suggested topics for conversation.

"I'm glad that's over," Wanda said after a while. "I don't know how or what they expected to find, but I am cleared to return to work – or rather, training to work."

"That's good," David said, playing along. "You never were the meek stay at home kind. What's going to happen if we have kids?"

"We get a nanny!" Wanda said right away. "I'll worry about that if I am silly enough to get pregnant. The important thing is that I won't be a liability if you are posted to some sensitive government department."

"As if! I'd be starting as somebody's gofer, I expect. And so, no doubt, will you."

"I don't know. I overheard some mention of making me nursemaid to Tanya."

"Well someone needs to teach her the language and how to be an American woman. So what did Rickard say?"

Wanda realised that the abrupt change of subject was because they had said all they wanted the listener to hear on the previous subject.

"He's pleased. He said the protein levels are very low. It seems the treatment he gave me is still working. Of course, I got the usual lecture – eat healthy, stay active. He has got some of his team trying to identify the gene that is causing it. Can't see the sense in that. Since he only knows a couple of people with the problem."

"So things are looking up," David finished, and he turned on the CD-player for a while.

Chapter 17

Tanya arrived at the cottage within half an hour of them getting back. She greeted them both with hugs.

"I have been so alone since you went off," she admitted in her mixed language. "The day you left, I woke up with a frightful cold. I finally went and saw the doctor and he gave me something that made me dopey. I think I slept most of the last few days – but I feel good today."

David shook his head. "I only got bits of that."

Wanda had understood all of it, but suggested, "Could you talk in Russian so David can practice that language? He can't follow that mixed patois of yours."

"How is your father?" Wanda asked her in English.

"Oh – him. He has been frightfully busy preparing for his meeting with the American scientists," Tanya commented. "I haven't seen him for days. I didn't want to give him my cold. Today he is busy talking to Mr Goldman. I might not exist – I might as well have stayed in Russia."

"No, I'm glad you are here," Wanda said at once. Tanya felt a bit like a sister. "Let him get the meeting over with first."

"He has never had time for me," Tanya complained.

"I think he did. He wanted you to come with him."

"That is only because he felt guilty for not being able to help my mother." Tanya's resentment was palpable. "Anyway, did you know that they are holding the meeting here, instead of taking father to Washington?"

"No," Wanda lied. "I haven't been around and no one thought to mention it. Why?"

"They didn't want to transport him – in case someone tried to kill him again. They say he will be safer here."

"So, when is this happening?" Wanda asked to distract herself from what she had tried to do.

"The day after tomorrow," David supplied. "Anyway Tanya, Wanda and I have to talk to Addison. She has to help with the security detail – since she has worked in that area before. I will probably tag along."

Tanya went off without a fuss. Wanda stared after her for a moment. The conversation had raised many questions in her mind that she didn't want to ask David yet. She waited until they were freshening up after their trip, in preparation to seeing Addison. With the water running, she asked David, "Is this cottage bug-free?"

David nodded. "I check frequently. And I am sure no one has been in since I left to get you."

Another trick, Jim hadn't missed. Like ensuring that Tanya was kept away from her father. She wondered why. Was it just in case Tanya was also programmed to kill him? Wanda told herself to forget such notions in case Tanya picked them up from her mind.

"Have you seen my iPod?" Wanda asked as they were about to leave the cottage. "I thought I put it in the front room."

"You don't need it now!" David told her. "I'll help you look for it later."

Wanda shrugged and followed her husband out the door. It annoyed her that she didn't know where it was. She remembered putting it on the table, but David was right. She didn't need it – just wanted it.

"That must be the best thing I have ever got for you," David teased. "You have hardly let it out of your sight."

"It's nice to listen to when I can't listen to you," Wanda retorted with a grin. "Besides, if I get stuck with Matheson, I'd rather listen to that than him."

David chuckled softly. "Don't be like that, it's unprofessional. Anyway, I think Matheson's problem is that he is a doctor not an administrator. He's out of his depth with all this military stuff."

"If he can't handle the military stuff he shouldn't be a military doctor," Wanda suggested softly.

"Anyway, Addison wants you to check the security with him. You shouldn't have to deal with the good doctor."

"Yeah, but have you noticed that Addison has been a yo-yo lately? Away more than he is here?"

David didn't reply. He had noticed that and had the sudden thought that when they got to this meeting, the General wouldn't be there.

He was almost right.

"My apologies, David, Mrs Martin – er – Wanda," Addison said after he had invited them into his office. "I've been called away. Mr Goldman and Dr Matheson will be in charge of things for me."

Addison hurried out. Wanda sent an "I was right" glance at David before turning her attention to the two men.

Goldman addressed them. "A change of plan, David. Professor Krinsky has asked for an assistant to help him prepare his presentation. You've done that sort of thing before, I believe?"

"Yes," David agreed, but his name hadn't been David Martin back then.

"Good. Wanda, you'll be working with Dr Matheson. I understand you are a security expert."

Wanda was sure Goldman was not exactly poking fun at her – but was definitely aware of her former life.

"Yes, Sir, I am," Wanda agreed, inwardly amused at the flash of disbelief that crossed Matheson's face.

"I would have thought you a bit young to be an expert," Matheson said aloud.

She smiled at him. "Have you figured out how I got off the base that time?"

Matheson's face flushed red.

Wanda relented. "I probably started learning about security systems at the age you were when you started medicine. It is a much easier subject to master than medicine. And since you had more important things to learn about, I'm glad to help."

Matheson forced an agreeable smile onto his face. "Fine then, perhaps you could teach me a few things. I will organise a car and driver to take us around."

Wanda merely nodded. She would have preferred to walk. There would be less chance of missing something that way. Well, she could always do that later – on her own.

David waved at Wanda as he went off towards the secure area where Stefan Krinsky was now housed. Goldman and two marines went with him.

As he walked, he mused that Jim's strategy was, as usual, close to brilliant. Wanda would be out in the open where any enemy agent that sought to use her could approach. He didn't know all the details of the plan but he expected to learn more shortly when he was "helping Stefan Krinsky".

One thing he knew for sure and he felt sure Wanda didn't know, was that the real Stefan Krinsky was not on the base. Jim himself was impersonating the Russian scientist, who had been secreted out while both Wanda and Tanya were unconscious in the detention cells. Tomorrow though, another of Jim's people would be playing that role. Someone who understood the science and could present it and answer questions. Jim was going to be needed to be seen as himself.

David pushed those thoughts away. He had his own job to do. When he entered the Professor's room, he must act as if he were speaking to the real scientist.

The marines waited outside the room. David and Goldman entered.

"Good afternoon, Professor," Goldman greeted. "I have brought you the assistant you requested. This is David Martin. I believe you have met?"

"Yes. Yes indeed. Can you type, young man?"

David nodded. "Yes, Sir. What do you need done?"

Goldman excused himself.

"I hope you can read my writing," the Professor seemed distracted. "I need these notes to be legible for my American associates."

David was aware that the door had not been closed properly. So it seemed was "Krinsky", for with his back to the door, he pointed to three places in the room, before walking to a table and picking up an untidy pile of notes.

David glanced at the pages and said, "Right, Sir. I think there will be no problem."

"Good! You can work…over there." Krinsky pointed to a desk near a window.

David heard the faint sound of the door being closed.

Krinsky followed him and pointed to the drawer in the desk. David opened it and saw a small earpiece. Krinsky indicated for David to put it in his ear.

David heard Wanda's and Matheson's voices. He nodded understanding that he was to listen to that too.

Krinsky wandered off to near one of the places that he had earlier pointed to and began muttering in a low voice. David studied the machine he was to use for typing. He had expected a computer, but this was only an electric typewriter that had word processing capacity. He found its on switch and paper.

As he worked, he realised that the typewriter was not as noisy as the old manual typewriters, but was noisier than a computer keypad. He guessed it was for the benefit of the listening device nearby. He grinned as he began to type, finding that the skills he had taught himself returned quickly. He didn't have to watch the keys, because he could touch type. He glanced every now and then about the room, watching the pacing of "Krinsky" and the doors and windows. He was alert for trouble. After about five minutes, he saw a slender dark skinned man enter the room from an adjoining one and go to two of the places "Krinsky" had pointed to. He fiddled briefly and held up two deactivated listening devices.

The third device was over near his typewriter. The dark man indicated that he would take over the typing. The transition was smoothly done. The noise of the typing paused only briefly. "Krinsky" gestured for David to come over to him.

The heavy accent dropped from the man's voice, and David recognised Jim's own voice. He had it pitched very low so the sound would not carry over the noise of the typing.

"David, one of the men you helped catch has talked," Jim came right to the point. "He claims that the people he is working for have someone on the base, though he doesn't know who it is or what he looks like. That must be how they knew where Stefan was to be. And it means someone relatively high up. We need to find who it is. Addison volunteered to step aside, since he must be considered suspect."

David shook his head, denying that point.

Jim went on, "I don't think so either, but he wants this cleared up. Now, we have to expect an attempt to be made on the Professor before tomorrow's meeting. We need to catch everyone involved."

David nodded and listened to Jim outline his plan and what David was to do and to be alert for. Then, using hand gestures, Jim sent David back to the typewriter and another smooth changeover occurred. The dark skinned man reconnected the two devices and withdrew to an adjoining room.

Wanda waited for Matheson to finish shuffling papers into a folder.

"Come on then," Matheson said finally.

Wanda followed him silently. Making no comment when he did not go directly to the front of the building where he had arranged for the car to wait. He went instead to the room where the guard positions were monitored.

While he went to talk to the men at the monitors, Wanda waited by the door, resisting the urge to clap a hand over her ear. Somehow she was hearing a high pitched squeal from the implant. It was giving her a headache and distracting her. She sensed Matheson returning and looked up. He seemed to be speaking to her, but the noise in her ear was making his words impossible to hear.

"Sorry, I didn't catch that. Too much noise," Wanda apologised when Matheson was close. He opened his mouth again.

Wanda didn't realise that her awareness was turned off. In that oblivious state, with radio static deafening the device in her right ear, Matheson whispered into the other ear.

"Who am I?" he asked. "Speak quietly."

"Oliver," Wanda whispered without realising it.

"What must you do?"

"I must obey your instructions," Wanda answered.

"Good. Draw me a square."

Matheson gave her a pen and a small pad of paper.

Wanda drew, not a square, but a circle. Matheson smiled. That had been a test to see if the commands had been removed.

"Good. I am instructing you to make no mention of any security breach in the west fence while we are inspecting the perimeter. When we get back to the office, you will only tell about the way you got out of the eastern fence. Nod if you understand?"

Wanda nodded.

"You will remember nothing from the time you entered this room until now."

Wanda was aware again, trying to hear Matheson who gestured out of the room.

"All guard positions report quiet," Matheson told Wanda. "As we drive around, look for anything that you think needs investigating – and when we get to your escape point, tell me."

Wanda grinned as she followed Matheson to the black SUV. The marine driver was standing by the car, waiting for them.

In front of the dark man, whose name was Brendan Collins, was a brief case sized screen with a picture outlining the base. A green light blinked in a position inside one of the buildings – this was Jim still acting as Krinsky. An orange light had moved to be outside the admin building where David and Brendan both knew Wanda was getting into the car with Matheson. This light moved along the road and onto the perimeter road where it turned left. David was concentrating on what he was hearing through the transmitter in Wanda's ear.

Jim gestured a signal meaning "got anything?" David shook his head. He was no longer typing but a tape was playing near the remaining working "bug" so any listener would still be hearing typing and the occasional mutter from the professor.

"Matheson went via the radio room," David said softly to Jim. "I had a lot of feedback through the microphone."

Brendan nodded; he was listening through earpieces joined by a narrow metal band that fitted over his head. He was also recording everything.

The orange light stopped at the first gate. David reported, "Matheson has told Wanda to get out and look around. He is giving the guards their instructions and telling them to be extra vigilant."

As the inspection continued, Wanda said very little. When they went along the eastern fence, Wanda showed Matheson where she had got out and how. Matheson arranged for extra guards to be placed there and for the tree overhanging the fence to be cut back.

Along the north fence, Wanda mentioned two vulnerable places. One was the emergency gate, which was seldom used and usually securely locked.

"Short work for bolt cutters," Wanda said bluntly.

Matheson summoned guards for there too. He ordered a team to fill in a water channel or animal burrow that had left a possible way under another part of the fence.

They worked around the fence stopping at each gate, Matheson instructing the guards while Wanda studied the security set up.

At the western gate, when Wanda passed close to two of the men, she sneezed twice in quick succession.

In the room where Jim watched, Brendan beckoned to Jim and pointed to the position and held up two fingers.

"Not the east fence," Jim said softly. "Notify Aldrin, and get Addison to send half of his men around to the west."

Brendan nodded, just as a low buzz startled both men. He picked up the screen and went into the other room.

David realised that the buzzer was a warning. Jim pointed to the tape and David quickly stopped it and hid the player in a drawer. He sat back at the typewriter and stretched as if taking a break.

Jim had become, once again, the perfect replica of Stefan Krinsky, but was standing where David could help protect him. Both heard the code knock on the door, and stopped seeming to talk together to look at the door.

David stood in alarm and Jim pretended to be startled and frightened as masked armed men entered the room.

"Do as we say and you won't get hurt," one of the four men said in English.

A second masked man came over to David who looked to have been caught in the act of drawing a weapon, as if paralysed by the sight of the bigger automatic weapon aimed at him. His gun was wrenched from him and jammed into that man's belt. And then, the man reversed his weapon and brought the butt down on David's head. David had stared as if in disbelief and crumpled under the blow. He fell with his eyes closed and a bleeding scalp wound.

During this time, a third man checked the adjoining room, and reported, "Clear."

"What is the meaning of this," Krinsky demanded, looking at the fallen David, and dithering about going to help him and not moving.

"Come with us Professor," the main speaker ordered and two of the others came up behind him and gave him a shove. When he started to refuse, they grabbed his wrists and tied them with a plastic zip tie and gagged him.

"If you try to escape, we will shoot," Krinsky was told,

Wanda knew when the attempt to kidnap Stefan Krinsky began. She sensed a surge of emotion from David. They were being driven down the last stretch of the fence.

"They are attacking the Professor," Wanda said suddenly, surprising Matheson.

Matheson wasted a moment, turning to stare at Wanda, and then snapped a command to drive there. The car accelerated and sped back to the building, arriving just as the security alarms began.

"Watch here," Matheson ordered the driver. He ran into the building, pulling a gun from his jacket. Wanda followed, more cautiously as she was not armed.

Matheson had stopped just inside, and was glancing around. They both heard the sound of booted feet approaching. Wanda was expecting to see the security guards responding to the alarm, and guessed Matheson was waiting for them before acting.

Privately she was wondering how Matheson had the guts to even enter the building where he might have to act against men with superior numbers and weapons.

Wanda had fewer qualms and was about to go and see what was happening when Matheson uttered what sounded like a curse.

Wanda stopped, oblivious to everything. Matheson whispered in her ear, "Get Stefan Krinsky and take him out to the car. Come on, you are now awake."

Wanda saw Matheson moving forward and followed him. They saw the infiltrators, still masked, when they turned into the passage. The intruders fired silenced weapons, Wanda ducked, but the shots had missed them both. Matheson returned fire and ducked back out of the way. He glanced back into the passage, saw the intruders retreating and moved after them. Wanda followed, keeping to the side of the passage, and low. She saw Krinsky tripping and falling just as a challenge was heard from somewhere ahead, and more shooting.

Matheson opened a side door and moved and grabbed Krinsky when no ne seemed to be looking. He dragged the Russian back and shoved him into the room. To Wanda he said, "Stay here and keep quiet. When it is safe, get him out."

The room was a supply closet and had little free space within. Wanda pushed Krinsky further in and jammed the door. She then put her ear to the wood and listened to the commotion in the passage, and was oblivious to the attempts of the man with her to get her attention.

"WANDA!" Jim thought as strongly as he could. He couldn't talk and she didn't seem aware of his nudging. Nor did she respond to his thought as she sometimes did.

He wasn't greatly worried; even though he was sure she was currently under some compulsion. The infiltrators seemed to want Krinsky alive. Matheson, in the passage and close to the door was giving instructions for a search.

Jim recognised Aldrin's voice and Matheson directed him out the back way. After a few minutes, the passage was quiet. Wanda opened the door when quiet knocking suggested it was now safe.

Matheson helped her walk the professor out. He released the gag but claimed to have nothing to cut the wrist bindings.

"We need you away from here, Sir," Matheson spoke to the man he believed to be Krinsky. "We'll go to the infirmary. Wanda, check outside make sure the way is clear."

Wanda didn't question what she was doing. She obeyed Matheson and a few moments later returned and gestured them forward.

They went out to the waiting car, and then Matheson suddenly exclaimed, "What are you doing? Put that gun down!"

Wanda saw the driver aiming a weapon at them and suddenly needed to sneeze. She sneezed again almost immediately. In that moment of distraction, she didn't see the man that came up from behind her, and tapped Krinsky on the head. Before she could react, Matheson told her quietly, "Do nothing."

The unconscious Krinsky as bundled into the trunk of the car. The second man backed away, leaving the driver putting his weapon away.

Matheson whispered a word in Wanda's left ear and then leaned into the car and began issuing orders by radio.

Wanda heard him warning guard posts about a vehicle that had Krinsky in it.

Inside the room where the professor had been, David had gone at once to look for Brendan. His head wound was minor as he had seen the blow and dropped under it.

Brendan emerged from a cupboard and had the screen up again.

"He's doing everything that he should do if he is loyal," David remarked, referring to Matheson. He knew Brendan was hearing the transmission too. They heard him report a car heading towards the west gate. "He thinks Stefan is in it." David said checking the screen. Both the orange and green dots were still just outside the building.

The dots began to move. Brendan spoke into a microphone mouthpiece. "Willie, Jim is not in the first car – he is in another – Possibly driven by or with Matheson in it."

In the car, Wanda believed they were following another car, the one with Krinsky in it, towards the west gate. When they got there, they saw chaos. The gate had been smashed and four guards lay on the ground. Through the gate, about one hundred meters down the road, a black car had crashed into a tree.

Matheson got out, as did Wanda.

"Drive down and block the road," Matheson ordered his driver. He then turned his attention to the injured men. Two had been shot and the other two seemed to have been knocked down. These were starting to try and sit up.

Wanda left the injured to Matheson and went into the guard post for a first aid kit. Leaving that with Matheson, she scanned the area. The driver had parked Matheson's car and was examining the wreck.

"There's no one in it," the man called.

Matheson spoke to Wanda, "Have him check the boot!"

Wanda yelled the command. She heard traffic on one of the guard's radios, listened and reported to Matheson.

"Gate 4 and gate 6 have been breached. One car was stopped, the other got away," Wanda told Matheson.

"Get onto Goldman," Matheson ordered. "He can handle this now. I have more important things to do."

Wanda went into the guard house and asked for Goldman. She told him the situation and that Matheson was dealing with injured men. She was told that help would be on the way and local authorities would be alerted to help search for the escapees.

Wanda turned her attention to the less injured men; they were not too badly hurt, probably only bruised. She looked up from one of them and saw Colonel Aldrin and another man near Matheson's car. The driver, who had been leaning against it, straightened up and looked more alert. Wanda had a flash of warning. Her danger sense had just kicked in; she didn't think the trouble was near her, but at the car, for it had woken when she had looked there. She stood without realising it and began to run towards the car. Aldrin was asking the driver to open the trunk of Matheson's car. "What?" she said to herself, and then the truth occurred to her. "He's in there! The driver is going to shoot." She didn't realise she had spoken aloud.

David heard her words and snapped a warning. "The driver is part of this."

Brendan spoke the warning to Willie. They both heard two shots and stared at each other in fear until Aldrin's voice was heard. "He's here. He's okay."

Willie heard the warning in his earpiece and moved behind the driver. Aldrin caught sight of the driver's stealthy movement and acted. He hit the man's arm as he fired and the shots went into the ground, not into the trunk. Willie grabbed the driver and took his gun as Aldrin wrenched open the trunk. The driver, who was cradling his arm, gaped at the Colonel's strength. It felt like Aldrin had broken his arm.

"He's here. He's okay."

Aldrin gently lifted the man from the trunk. He was conscious and so Aldrin helped him to his feet and did something to release his wrists.

Wanda reached the man and touched is arm. "Are you alright?"

Her eyes met those of the man. "Jim!" she mouthed silently. With her mind wondering how she had not sensed this deception, she noticed his make up coming adrift. "I think you should go and rest," Wanda said. Her eyes signalled the reason to Jim.

Aldrin offered to drive him back. Wanda was tempted to go along, but Jim whispered, "Check everyone here."

Wanda glanced around, taking in the situation anew. Where were the men from the crashed car? Matheson hadn't sent anyone looking for them, and it would be dark soon. She decide not to bother him, instead she vocalised, knowing David would hear her. "No one has started looking for the men in the first car. Matheson thinks there were four of them."

A short time later a squad of marines raced out through the gate. They passed close to her and as they passed, Wanda sneezed. When she went past the now secured driver, she sneezed again. She sneezed twice when she returned to the now standing guards that had been knocked down.

Wanda asked how the men were, and suggested they sit and let the doctor check them. Both claimed to be fit enough to continue their shift and seemed not to think her advice of merit.

The man who had been with Aldrin was shadowing Wanda, and now he added his advice to hers. He did manage to convince them to return to the infirmary to be checked.

Willie winked at Wanda as the two guards began to walk with him towards the base. She had the sudden hunch he was one of Jim's men. That led her to realise that Jim must have expected this attempt. She shrugged back at the man – the attempt had almost succeeded.

Wanda assisted Matheson when he asked her. He kept her busy until Aldrin returned with extra guards and medics and stretchers in a truck. He oversaw the securing of the area, and spoke to the returning marine searchers.

With the patients readied for transport, Wanda sidled over to listen to the marines reporting to Aldrin. They had found no trail to follow. The men had just disappeared.

Near one of the men, she sneezed. Aldrin glanced at her and made a suggestion, "You might as well go back to your place, before that cold of yours gets worse."

"Thanks," she agreed, not sorry to go, though she expected they would want to debrief her when things quietened down.

Chapter 18

Matheson saw his patients settled into the infirmary. The two with bullet wounds had been airlifted to the nearest hospital for surgery, the two that had been knocked down were resting. He went into his office and sat to consider the afternoon's events.

He had failed to get Krinsky out. Certain people would be angry with him.

At least no one seemed to suspect his part in the attempted abduction. Goldman had praised his efforts. If he had been suspicious, he'd be in detention now.

Matheson's face twisted into a wry grimace. He had fooled those listening via that woman's earpiece. Goldman didn't realise he knew about that.

He considered his next move – although he wished he hadn't let himself be compromised into helping.

His phone rang. From the tone of the bell, it was an internal call.

"He still lives!" a voice whispered through the phone. "He must die! You have two weapons. Use them. If you fail again, you will die."

Paul Matheson shivered. He knew that voice and knew to take the warning seriously. He hadn't ever seen the man's face, but who ever the man was – he was here, on the base – unrecognised.

Even though he wanted no further part in this, Matheson knew he had no choice.

The guards at the entrance to the security section let him through. Had he not been the acting Director of the base he would have been denied access. He was announced to the occupants of this suite of rooms by the guards at Krinsky's door. "Doctor Matheson is here, Mr Goldman."

"Send him in," the disembodied reply came through the radio.

The weapons that had been ready for use, were lowered and the door opened from inside.

Matheson was confronted by two Stefan Krinskys.

"What is going on here?" he asked harshly.

One of the two men began to peel off a layer of plastiskin moulded with Krinsky's features. Jim Phillips was revealed.

"Sorry for the deception, Paul," Jim said at once.

Goldman continued. "We had a tip off that an attempt was to be made to abduct Stefan." He nodded at the other man, who had remained seated as if in shock.

"We allowed the attempt to proceed," Jim said, indicating the disguise as if that was sufficient explanation.

"Any word of those that escaped?" Matheson asked.

"The car was found and two men were arrested," Goldman told him. "They will be questioned. The marine driver assigned to you is being detained here. He isn't talking. I think, Paul, that you were very lucky."

Matheson looked startled. "They wouldn't have wanted me," he uttered, glancing from Goldman to Phillips and back.

"You might have been in the way," Jim explained. "However, they failed this time and I think we got all the people involved."

"We must still maintain tight security for tomorrow," Goldman insisted. "We've foiled two attempts to get him – we must assume they will try again."

"Yes, you are correct. What do you require of me?" Matheson straightened his posture.

"All the scientists will be arriving tomorrow morning," Goldman reminded him. "I will need you to help me greet them. We will need to be tactful because some will not approve of the security measures. I have put Colonel Aldrin in charge of security and he will have metal detectors and x-ray screening machines in place. How are the injured guards?"

"Both are resting," Matheson reported. "I will advise you when I have heard from the hospital."

"Good," Goldman said, as if his mind had moved to other matters.

There was a lull in the conversation and Stefan Krinsky spoke up. "Mr Goldman, I would like to see my daughter. She can't have missed all the commotion and she will be worried."

Matheson had been purposely avoiding glancing at the scientist, but his request gave him a reason. He still couldn't fathom what was so important about the man. Or why certain people really wanted him.

"She's fine, Stefan. I sent David over to see her and tell her you are safe and were never really in danger."

"My thanks, many thanks," Krinsky muttered.

Matheson excused himself and left the room. He walked away past the two door guards in a very thoughtful mood. Goldman and that man Phillips, whoever he was, had been too dammed lucky. However, he was running out of time and options.

Back in his office, he sat in his chair and mused. Those that now owned his soul had several more nasty surprises available - if the gas grenades he'd planted in that room did not work. He needed to set up one of them now – while all the main opponents were congratulating themselves on their cleverness.

He woke up his computer and plugged in the microphone he used to record his reports. When it was ready he spoke crisply and clearly into the device. That annoying female had obeyed him today and would be useful tomorrow. Everyone thought she was clear of coercion. He'd make use of that.

When he finished speaking, he moved the voice file to another location and connected another device to his computer. He synchronised this with the stored file.

When that was finished he disconnected both the microphone and the other device and erased the voice file from the computer. He changed the program to his medical reports program.

The second device went into his pocket and he went for a walk.

In the security section, once Matheson had left the room and been reported heading back to his office, "Stefan Krinsky" was on his feet and examining every place that Matheson might have touched in the room.

Goldman and Jim kept talking of the days events and plans for the following day, but were also watching the other man.

Brendan Collins, now playing the role of Krinsky, pointed to a listening device. He continued looking and found two more devices. He placed a hand over his face, miming that they were gas grenades. Goldman and Jim exchanged sombre glances.

"I'll take my leave, Stefan," Jim said in a normal voice. "I'll see you tomorrow. David will have all the notes typed and copied for you."

He left the room and spoke to the guards while the door was ajar. Those in the room heard clearly the instructions he gave to the door guards – two of his men.

Any listener would be sure that Stefan was not going to leave that room. Before the others left, Brendan set up a tape playing the sounds that a lone occupant might make.

When they were all out in the passage and the door was locked, Jim spoke to his men, warning them of the smoke grenades and instructing them to report if they were set off.

Chapter 19

Wanda was stalking around inside the cottage when David arrived back. It was full night and she was feeling excluded.

"Why do I feel like you are somewhat annoyed?" David asked with a sigh.

"Because I am!" Wanda muttered. "Matheson sent me back like a useless nobody. I though at least, Jim would want a report."

"He does," David assured her. "Now that the dust has settled. We caught six agents that had substituted for real marines. And, we were listening to everything you were saying or heard. Jim wants you to keep a low profile for a bit. Oh, and here!"

Wanda glanced at her husband as he pulled something from his pocket. She recognised her iPod.

"Where was it?"

"Just outside the door. You must have been blind!"

Wanda said nothing. It had not been there when she went out or returned. Of that, she was certain. "Someone must have found it and returned it," she finally suggested.

David shrugged. "Ok, now, let me get the recorder and you can tell Jim all you think he needs to know. In your usual thorough and tactless style."

Wanda snorted, but felt less annoyed. "Ok. Just let me get a drink first. This will be thirsty work."

She gestured around the room, implying that David should check again for bugs. He did, and gave her the 'all clear' thumbs up.

David didn't prompt Wanda; just let her tell things her way. If Jim wanted clarification of anything, he would ask later. But, listening to Wanda he marvelled at the detail she put into the report. He kept quiet when part of her narrative, was unexpectedly summarised by comparison.

Mostly, what she was saying agreed with what he had heard through the transmitter implant. Except, he felt it wasn't quite right. For instance, she should have sensed that it was Jim with her, not Krinsky. And there was a time when she hadn't heard Jim talking to her.

These insights were the reason why he was debriefing her, not Jim. He, David, was the one person that knew her implicitly.

Wanda's snide comments about Matheson he first put down to their mutual antipathy. Matheson had sounded loyal, and acted loyal, but he was beginning to agree with Jim and Goldman that Matheson had to be involved. Though if he was, would he have stayed after that failure today? He had brazened it out – which took nerve – and he must think now that he had fooled everyone.

When Wanda finished, David told her to get some sleep. "I won't be back for ages yet, and Jim wants you fresh for tomorrow. He will brief you then."

Wanda hugged him and let him go. She was tired. When the door closed behind him, she began listening to her iPod, to let the music relax her.

It was very late when David returned to the cottage – or rather very early next morning. His mind was full of the briefing for the following day and he was too tense to sleep. He found Wanda's iPod beside her bed and decided to listen to the music for a time. As he sat in one of the lounge chairs, trying to relax, he was suddenly aware that the music had changed to a voice speaking. He tensed and listened. He stopped the voice, glanced at the IPod's screen and memorised the name of the voice file. And then he stalked out of the cottage and over to where Jim would be spending the night.

Jim had only just fallen asleep, but when he opened his door to David, he knew the matter was important.

Inside, he listened with growing disquiet, and thought quickly.

"Can you download that file to a USB?" Jim asked David. "I'll get Doug Lang here by morning, have him listen to it and see what he can do. I will have him talk to Wanda as soon as he gets here."

"I'll download it and check if there is more of it on there," David promised. Then he had a revelation. "She had the IPod in the detention cell – after Mattheson cleared it. That had to be what set her off – and it had to be Mattheson."

"It looks like it," Jim agreed. "But not a word about it. He thinks he is in the clear and that I didn't notice the oddities in the reports of the attack."

Doug Lang arrived just as the sky was beginning to lighten in the east. Jim met him at the gate and took him to Wanda and David's cottage.

David heard their quiet entry and came to greet them. He took them to the front room.

"Good work, David," Lang said in greeting. "I listened to those files on the way here. I think I can do something with them. Before I start, though, I need to get a feel for how Wanda's ESP works. Jim thinks that whoever hypnotised her doesn't, can't, know about it. I want to use that talent and link it to suggestions I implant. I hope that it will provide a - pause – in her mind before she acts on an enemy implanted instruction. Give her time to switch to one of ours."

David looked interested. "What do you want to know?"

"Tell me about her. Jim has told me a lot – but you have known her more intimately. What sort of person is she? What are her core values? How far can she be pushed against her will? What things make her act?"

David sat down and collected his thoughts. When he began to talk, Doug listened intently, correlating David's thoughts with his own impressions and those of Jim Phillips.

When David ran out of things to say, Doug asked, "Tell me about when you first met her?"

"I wasn't David Martin then," David said, and he related their meeting – when Wanda was running to help her sister and hiding from the same people that were chasing him.

"All you have told me suggests that she is not one to stand by if she can help save a life. That's promising. It also shows that she won't – deep down – want to take a life."

"Unless, it was the most merciful thing," David whispered, remembering a moment when Wanda had admitted in assisting such an act.

"She wouldn't choose to shoot someone in cold blood," Jim stated. He looked as if he were remembering something. David could think of no incident that he might be referring to. His face was thoughtful.

Jim saw his look. "I encountered her, at a time before she had even began working for the Franklins. She had been running with a wild bunch that were just branching out – moving up – from petty crime and vandalism. I saw her face down the leader, who would have shot a man, would have shot me – to protect us."

"Wanda never mentioned that," David said thoughtfully.

"I doubt that she knew it was me," Jim admitted. "I was using another name."

David guessed that he was also disguised at the time. "She impressed you even then," David suggested.

Jim nodded. "That's why I think, I hope, Doug can help her. Why don't you wake her? We are running out of time."

Wanda was awake and dressed, and seeming to be meditating on the edge of the bed.

"Time for me?" she asked David. They both knew she was aware of the guests.

David nodded. "Scared?" he asked.

Wanda retorted defiantly. "I'm never scared!"

"No – you just never show it. It's not the same."

Wanda grinned wryly at him, admitting his point. "I don't like not being in control of myself. But next to you, I trust Jim above anyone else. This will work!"

David wished he could be as positive. He was glad when Jim took him away so Wanda and Doug could talk. They had things to do in the conference room before the meeting started.

"Why are you here?" Wanda asked abruptly after David and Jim had left.

Doug Lang answered directly. "David found some odd files on your IPod. Voice, not music. We believe it was the cause of your abhorrent behaviour in the detention section."

"O…Kay. And?" Wanda prompted.

"And I can use those files to negate that trigger that the people implanted in your mind."

"That sounds promising, but there might be others?"

"I would assume so," Doug told her bluntly. "However, I also intend, with your assent, to add some compulsions of our own – and to use hypnosis to reinforce some of your personal core values."

"I hate this!" Wanda exploded quietly. "I hate having someone else in control of my mind."

"You let Franklin do it," Doug reminded her.

Wanda said nothing for a long moment. "OK. Not anymore."

"Good. Now were you listening to your music last night?"

"For a while," Wanda admitted. "What were they trying to make me do this time?"

"Get at Stefan," Doug told her. "However, I can use that trigger to get you under – and working from there, cancel the hypnotic suggestions. Are you ready?"

Wanda took a calming breath and nodded.

Doug turned on a music player and played a few bars of a tune. He saw an instant change in Wanda. Her eyes took on a blank look, but she also seemed more attentive.

Doug set to work, learning all he could from her and then making her forget it.

Whilst Wanda was still oblivious, he took her mind right back to that time Jim had mentioned – reinforcing her core value – that life was precious – that she did not kill.

"The next time that you hear this tune, or the name Oliver, you will sneeze three times and you will remember what is said and trust your instincts to tell you if you should obey."

Doug played the tune again as he mentioned it and then again when he had finished speaking. Wanda sneezed three times.

Wanda saw Doug Lang – now seated opposite her and recalled that he had been standing an instant ago.

"So – are you done? Am I cured?"

"You shouldn't respond to Matheson, and if he tries anything you will recall it," Doug assured Wanda.

"Mattheson!" Wanda shook her head. "Was he behind it all?"

"I don't think so. He's more likely a pawn, just as you are."

"Damn! That means that there is still someone out there… will I be able to keep working for Jim?"

"You are working for him now. But – in answer to your question – we still need to wait until this matter is over."

Wanda didn't need to be told that it depended on the unknown agent and if he still had a hold on her.

"Is there anything I can do?" Wanda asked.

Doug was thoughtful. He had given her instructions under hypnosis, but…

"Yes. There is. Jim is thinking of having a fake Stefan Krinsky deliver the talks. That fake Stefan must be protected. He must not be killed."

"I don't want to kill the real one either!" Wanda told him tartly. "Anything else?"

"Trust your instincts," Doug told her.

"I usually do."

"Then, that's all we can do for now. After this is over, I will give you a course of anti-hypnotic conditioning. It should make you more resistant to hypnosis in future."

"Perfect. Where does Jim want me?"

"Conference room," Doug told her. "Off you go,"

Jim met the rest of his agents in the conference room which had been sealed off since the previous night. Willie and Paris, with Brendan's help – had erected a false wall in two corners and set up a video monitoring system and other safeguards. They had then done a thorough check of the room for sabotage, bombs and other nasty surprises.

"The place is secure," Brendan reported. "Willie and Zandercan cover the whole room. The vents will enable them to shoot if needed."

Jim glanced at the false walls; the vents were set above the level of peoples heads.

"The equipment?" he asked.

"All working. Spares are in the drawer under the projector," Brendan confirmed.

"Fine. Go get ready, Brendan. Aldrin will be watching you. Send Zander back here when he is done with you. Willie – you get into position now. David, you watch Wanda – just in case. This is the last chance for the enemy to get at Stefan. We must identify the top agent. They think Wanda is one of their weapons – so they may be watching her. If it seems that Matheson's control of her is gone, the top agent may try to activate her himself. Keep listening to what comes through the implant."

"Who will be watching Tanya," David asked.

"I'll have her with me. But I will tell Wanda to watch her too. Goldman will be watching Matheson."

David considered that Jim had everything covered.

"The guests are due to arrive in an hour," Jim went on. "None of them are real scientists, but all will have been well briefed and will be convincing. David, you can tell Wanda that. She will probably sense it. I don't want her to make a scene about it."

David nodded.

"Okay. We are done in here. We will wait in the ante-room." Jim instructed.

Chapter 20

The guests were arriving. Matheson quelled his inner agitation, realising that he had to wait to finish Krinsky. Still – he had the Martin woman. Perhaps she would act before he needed to. He hadn't been able to get near her since she had shown up. But – he didn't need to. She had her IPod earpieces in, annoying woman. She would be getting his message. He forced a smile on his face and went to greet the first arrivals.

He shook hands with each one and introduced himself, also inviting them to partake in the light refreshments.

One questioned the security procedures, seeming to be indignant at needing to walk through a metal detection system and have his briefcase checked.

Goldman had remained silent and watchful.

"That's everyone," Goldman said quietly to Matheson when the twelfth guest had arrived. "Have them go into the Conference room, Tell them that Krinsky will arrive soon."

Tanya Krinsky arrived at that time, and came over to Wanda. "Where is my father? I want to see him."

"Coming," Wanda told her, as she tried to sense her friend's thoughts. All she sensed was the desire to see her father.

Jim gestured with his head. Wanda was to escort the scientists into the other room and try to sense if any deceptions were being played. It was possible that some of the decoys may have been replaced.

Two marine guards emerged from the room and opened the doors fully. They then took a position on either side of the door.

Jim moved to stand next to Tanya. She did not seem aware of him; she was looking around as if to spot her father.

Wanda glanced back at her. Jim had warned that Tanya might also be under some compulsion, but she seemed normal so far. Still – Krinsky wasn't there yet. As soon as he arrived, Tanya should be able to tell if it was her father or not. Jim would have allowed for that.

Wanda interrupted the conversation of the first little huddle of scientists and invited then to enter the conference room.

"Your places are marked and Professor Krinsky will be here soon.

"Thank you, Mrs Martin," one identified her from her security pass. Those four men moved towards the open doors. David was there to direct them further.

Wanda moved to the second group. One of these asked directions to the men's room. She summoned a marine guard to escort him.

One of the second group commented on her likeness to Tanya Krinsky. Wanda felt a mild electric shock as the man seemed to accidentally brush against her. She heard a low voice say, "Replace the globe in the projector when it blows." She did not feel the object slipped into her pocket. "Use this one. If you feel this sensation again, you will shoot Stephan Krinsky."

Wanda felt the electric shock again. "You will obey, but you will not remember this conversation."

Wanda believed that she answered at once. "Yes, I have noticed the resemblance. It is an odd coincidence. But I am American through and through. Please take your places."

None of the other two men remarked on the odd conversation. They may as well not have heard it.

Goldman was talking to a third group, and Wanda was headed to the last group when there was a flurry of activity at the other door. Krinsky had arrived.

"Father!" Tanya said loud enough to be heard. She ran to him and gave him a hug.

Wanda watched, still unable to touch Tanya's mind and was oblivious to the close scrutiny of the man she had spoken to moments earlier.

Instinctively, Wanda began to move towards Tanya. The man watching her, edged back casually and brushed her, with out seeming to. Wanda felt the tingling but didn't realise that she couldn't move.

"Say nothing. Make no movement." The voice spoke into the ear without the transmitter and was too low to be picked up.

Wanda was still concentrating on Tanya. "She hasn't noticed," Wanda thought to herself. Tanya's mind was still blank, but Wanda could see vague movements of her hand and wrist. Jim, back close to her would not be able to see them.

Wanda felt her danger sense kick in. She knew that Tanya must not be allowed to finish what ever she was doing. She tried to move, but couldn't.

What was happening? She had to stop Tanya.

"Tanya! NO!" she thought strongly. Tanya went tense, but after a moment the stealthy hand movement continued.

"Tanya, NO. That is not Stefan Krinsky. He is a fake! It is a trick. Wait!"

Wanda thought strongly at Jim. She pictured Tanya and thought, "Something in her hand."

Jim Phillips moved fast and caught Tanya's wrist. He plucked away the micro syringe. Jim glanced at Wanda, who found she could move again and forgot the moment of paralysis.

A marine squad was summoned by a gesture from Jim and came to shepherd Tanya from the room.

Krinsky watched his daughter's departure, seemingly oblivious to the danger he had been in. "Why did she have to leave?" he asked Stev Aldrin, in a halting and confused tone.

Jim spoke quietly to him and the Professor nodded and continued into the room.

David watched the whole scene from near the inner door. His eyes flicked from Wanda to the other people still in the anteroom. He had noticed the apparent coincidence of a particular scientist talking to Wanda and being near his wife during Tanya's attempt on her father and kept it in mind. Matheson, with Goldman keeping close to him, had not been near that man.

Jim gestured for Wanda to wait before entering the conference room. David took over her role of seeing all the guests to their assigned seats. He handed out note taking supplies and bottles of water.

"Timely warning," Jim told Wanda softly. "However you gave it. What did you sense?"

"Nothing, Jim. Tanya's mind was blank. She didn't even realise the man wasn't her father."

"Wasn't it?" Jim countered quickly.

Wanda was confused. "But I thought..."

Jim deliberately interrupted her thought. "It's a shell game – like magicians use. Have you sensed anything at all?"

"No. The guards are OK – I'm sure. The scientists – well – they are all busy playing at being scientists."

Jim gave a wry grin, but Wanda sensed he was worried.

"Keep alert," he told Wanda and they entered the inner room together.

Wanda moved away to be near David by the door. Stev Aldrin hovered near Stefan Krinsky. The Russian was on a low podium and was being introduced by Magnus Goldman. Jim was watching Matheson while Goldman was talking.

The seats were set behind tables so that all the men had a good view of Krinsky and the projector screen. Goldman descended from the podium and took a seat next to Matheson. Jim moved about the edge of the room, speaking to the four marine guards and finally stopping where he could watch the scientists from behind.

Krinsky began to speak. Wanda was certain that it wasn't the real Russian, but she continued to pretend that it was. The halting English was exactly that of the Russian – his whole manner – perhaps it really was him. He introduced his subject by referring to a number of related topics. His audience was listening intently.

Wanda felt herself go tense. Krinsky was getting to the crux of his work – to reveal the knowledge that some people would kill to keep secret.

She saw David scanning the room but everyone seemed to be paying compete attention to the speaker.

Krinsky picked up the remote control for the projector so that he could bring up the first slide. The room lights dimmed. The projector screen was bright for a second and then went dark.

Someone brightened the room lights as Krinsky muttered an apology. Wanda trotted to the podium to get a spare globe from the drawer, except that she took one from her pocket and used that one in the projector. The screen now glowed brightly. Wanda glanced at the man near the light switch. As she moved her glance away she caught the gaze of one of the scientists. She could not look away from him until he dropped his gaze.

The lights dimmed. Krinsky began speaking again, recapping his previous comments. Wanda moved from the podium but the eyes of the scientist bothered her. Her mind worked furiously to place where she had seen them before.

Krinsky was talking about the first slide, Wanda turned to look that way, saw Krinsky about to press the remote to change slides. Like lightning, her memory clicked. She had seen a man with those eyes in a photograph – of an enemy agent. The face was unfamiliar, the eyes were not. They had watched her change the globes.

"Don't," Wanda yelled as Krinsky's fingers pressed on the button.

Understanding showed on Krinsky's face – too late - she thought, but Stev Aldrin had moved too fast to see.

The projector exploded into a fury of fiery destruction – the force of the blast going back to where Krinsky and Aldrin had stood.

Wanda grabbed the nearest extinguisher and raced to the podium, relieved to see Aldrin and Krinsky crawling away and getting to their feet.

It had been Aldrin's quick reflexes that had saved them.

The audience had risen and moved back from the fire. They were grouped together near the door. Two of the four guards had gone for more extinguishers.

There was a lot of confusion. Goldman and Matheson were urging all the guests back. Two of the guards were using extinguishers on the fire.

In that chaos, four men moved their hands stealthily under their jackets.

Two shots rang out, and two men dropped handguns and grabbed at wrists creased by bullets. David, who had not stopped watching the scientists, moved to the side of a third man. He poked a gun of his own into that one's side.

"Take you hand out of your jacket and keep both where I can see them," he warned the man. David frisked the man and removed the gun that was in his waist band. He pushed the man to one side.

Goldman moved closer to Matheson, the fourth man. "Don't do it, Paul," he advised softly. "Leave the gun where it is." He removed that weapon.

The fire was finally out. Wanda put the now empty extinguisher down, and took in the scene around her. She had heard the shots, and seen the guards taking charge of the two injured men. Now she saw the guns on the floor and went to retrieve them.

As she stood up, she felt a tingling shock and someone was helping her to stand back up. She turned to thank the man and saw the eyes. Her mind froze and she didn't seem to be hearing what the man was saying to her. What was she meant to be doing? The words, "Kill Stefan Krinsky" echoed in her mind. Without conscious thought, she edged through the milling group to find the Professor.

That she was carrying two confiscated guns had alarmed no one, not even David until she lifted the one in her right hand to point at Krinsky.

"Wanda, don't do it," a voice spoke but the words had no meaning. The eyes were behind Krinsky watching, urging, "Kill Krinsky."

Wanda didn't even know she was edging forward, arm out stretched, hand tensed to fire. She didn't see Aldrin ready to yank Krinsky to one side, or Jim holding David back from going to disarm her.

"Wanda, don't do it," Jim repeated.

David's face revealed his anguish and his mind yelled at his wife to no avail. Why weren't they trying to stop her? He willed her not to shoot. If she did...He didn't want to think about what that would mean.

Wanda's fingers touched the Professor, who watched her with intent eyes and no sign of fear. Her special senses told her the truth. This Krinsky was a fake, a fraud.

The eyes burned into her mind, "Kill Stefan Krinsky."

He's a fake. A new voice echoed in her mind, "Protect the fake Stefan Krinsky."

Wanda's mind cleared. The eyes! They were the enemy. The man with the eyes had a gun out, ready to fire. She move her own hand fractionally – her hand tensed and the gun fired.

Jim wrenched the gun from Wanda's hand, then looked at his associate, Brendan Collins – the fake Stefan. He was still standing, but with his hand on a burn graze on his neck. He had turned around to see a man slumped on the ground, gun in hand.

David reached Wanda before she fainted.

Chapter 21

The room was cleared of people. The three gunmen and Matheson had been taken to the detention cells. Before the dead man was taken to the cool room off the base medical centre, Goldman had watched Jim pull off a layer of plastiskin that had disguised his face. It revealed the face of the man that Wanda had recognised the eyes of.

Brendan, with a sigh of relief, removed the plastiskin face of Krinsky. Willie and Zanderstood near the door, close to where Wanda refused to lift her face from David's chest.

"Did we get all of them?" Goldman asked and Jim Phillips nodded.

Wanda nodded also and David said, "Wanda believes so."

"Excellent. My commendations to everyone involved." Goldman gestured to Stev Aldrin. Stev moved and shook hands with Jim.

"It has been a pleasure to work with you, Mr Phillips."

Jim smiled and answered in an equally formal way. "And with you Colonel. When you speak to Stefan, assure him that Tanya will be well. I have a leading psychologist working with her."

"And Wanda," Stev Aldrin asked, glancing at her.

"Yes," Jim smiled a smile full of relief.

"Good. She is a damned fine agent. Perhaps we can work together again."

Aldrin gave a wave that was suggestive of a salute and turned to follow Goldman from the room.

Jim waited a moment before speaking. "Brendan, go get that wound attended to. Willie, Zandercan you clean up here and I'll catch up with you before you go."

To Wanda and David, Jim said, "We need to talk."

Wanda began to shake all over.

"Come to the cottage Jim. It will be easier there. I think Wanda is still in shock."

David, with Wanda still clinging to him, sat on the couch in the cottage.

Jim made use of one of the chairs.

"Tanya is going to be okay then," David asked. "Does she know what was going on?"

"I don't think so," Jim decided. "Doug is talking to her."

"It will be a shock if she realised what she almost did," Wanda said quietly, finally turning red-rimmed eyes from David. "She didn't want to live with her father, but I don't think she really hates him."

"I agree with you there, Wanda," Jim told her. "I am glad you were able to warn me about her."

"What do you mean?" David asked. "How did Wanda do that? I saw her just standing there as if frozen."

"At that moment, I felt like I was," Wanda told David. "That man, the one I ...must have done something to me. I couldn't move, or speak. But I was still aware of Tanya's mind. It felt blank. It was odd. She didn't seem to be aware that your man wasn't her father. I was so sure she would. When I saw her hand moving, I tried to yell with my mind, she didn't hear me this time. That's when I tried to reach you Jim."

"You did – and it was a very odd feeling indeed. What about later?"

Wanda knew when he meant.

She shook her head as if to clear it. "I remember changing the globe – from the spares in the drawer..."

David interrupted. "You didn't go to the drawer. You took the globe from your pocket."

Wanda considered that. "I don't recall that ... anyway, I looked up when I had done it and saw those eyes. They held me until they looked away. I recognised them, but I couldn't remember where I had seen them. That really bugged me. Then I saw them glance at Krinsky. That's when I remembered where I had seen them – in a photo Goldman showed me. I knew something was going to happen and I yelled."

"What about when you picked up the guns?" Jim prompted.

"I remember thinking they shouldn't stay on the floor and going to get them – then it's blank. Until I touched...what was his name?"

"Brendan," David supplied.

"I realised he was a fake – not the real Krinsky. I remember being told to protect the fake Stefan Krinsky. Everything was suddenly clear then. I saw the man with the eyes right behind Brendan and I knew he was going to shoot if I didn't."

"He did," Jim told Wanda. "Virtually the instant you did. His bullet just creased Brendan. Aldrin pulled him aside in time."

Wanda slumped back into David. "What happens now? I killed that man."

"There won't be any problem," Jim assured her soberly. "It was a justified defensive action. Also, that man was a dangerous assassin. A lot of people will be glad he is dead."

Wanda hid her face again. Jim looked concerned.

"What she didn't tell you, Jim," David tried to explain. "Is the degree of shock she experienced when she killed that man. Not just because she did, but because on some level, her mind was still linked to his – and that mind was suddenly silenced."

"I'll get over it," Wanda muttered. "I won't go to pieces next time."

Jim nodded, accepting her evaluation.

David changed the subject. "How did those agents get in? We checked them all, over and over."

"I think we will find that Matheson was involved there. He is being questioned now. I am happy to let Goldman handle those details. He could well have provided the identifications and weapons. I understand that the dead man had been on the base for some days. What still needs to be learnt is where the four men are that those men replaced, and that however is a job for the official investigators. Our job is done."

Wanda looked up. "I never liked Matheson. Right from the start he rubbed me the wrong way – but I never suspected him at all. So really, what good is this trick in my head?"

"A good agent needs to be a little bit psychic," Jim told her gently. "A hunch, a feeling, may be all that stands between success and failure – life or death."

"What if it fails me when I need it most? People could die."

"Have your hunches, your intuition, ever failed you yet?" Jim asked.

"No...but today I was looking out for the enemy and couldn't see them."

"Possibly because a good agent acts the part of his cover until it is time to act," Jim told her. "After today, I know I can trust your ability, Wanda. If that trick of yours warns you of danger, well and good. If it doesn't, then you are no worse off than other good agents who rely on their normal senses."

"Then I can still work for you?" Wanda asked Jim, her eyes pleading.

"Yes – most definitely," Jim assured her and saw her whole body relax. "There is one more condition though."

Wanda eyed him cautiously. "What?"

Jim smiled. "You and David have to take a holiday – together. You haven't really had a chance to be on your own – have you?"

He grinned wider as both Wanda and David shook their heads.

"What about Goldman wanting to investigate my mind tricks?" Wanda asked.

"There's plenty of time for that," Jim dismissed that with a waving gesture. "Besides. He wants to have both you and Tanya for that. And Tanya has a few issues to sort out first and I think she needs time to get to know her father again. So – there is no reason for anyone to stop the pair of you disappearing for a while. I will know how to find you."

"We'll be available," Wanda promised. "David has this thing about earning his keep."

"I know," Jim grinned again. "Have your holiday – we will discuss that later. For now, you both will be getting a basic retainer."

"And if we need more," Wanda said straight faced, "I'll become a professional mind reader."

"No way," David said, giving Wanda friendly shove. "I am not going to share you with anyone for a time."

Neither noticed when Jim let himself out.

End of A New Life - Part 1 Hidden Secrets

Wanda's story is continued in A New Life - Part 2 First Mission

NOVELS

WANDA: FROM BAD TO WORSE

If she was going to die young, like her mother, Gwen Willard was determined to die rich and she had very few years to do it. Her first step was to leave home. She met Hooch, who taught her some exciting and illegal skills. She was the Dracos lucky mascot until she came to the attention of the police. Then her uncanny knack for predicting trouble, warned her to flee to the city and change her name.

Life wasn't easy. She was 15, had little money and no regular job, but her new skills came in handy. Then she crossed the path of an evil and unscrupulous man and she didn't want him to have his way.

WANDA: CHOOSING CRIME

Wanda was free. She was never going back to jail. But she was homeless, almost penniless and Harrison Franklin had a long and vengeful memory.

Jim Phillips had a long memory too, and Wanda had saved his life. Could he save her from Franklin?

WANDA: RISKING LIFE TO LIVE

The euphoria of successful heists were what kept Wanda Dean alive. At 23, she was crime boss Harrison Franklin's top agent – well paid for absolute obedience. That's all that mattered. Until she met Mike Johnston and her boss ordered him killed. For that, the Franklins were going to pay. In Risking Life to Live, justice conflicts with loyalty and the penalty for betrayal is death.

ERIN: THE FORCING OF WISDOM

For years, Erin has used the intricacies of cyberspace to banish unwanted emotions. Others call what she does hacking, and her manipulations criminal, but now her skill was exceptional - in, out, traceless. She was wrong. Someone betrayed her.

Travis has dangerous plans. He needs an electronics expert – one he can coerce through fear. Erin was perfect.

With the inescapable threat of prison looming, Erin accepts his offer of sanctuary. When she realises his intentions, she is in too deep. But the terrifying of innocents is unforgivable. She cannot walk away. She is an empath and shares their distress. She has to help them, even if it means prison, and insanity…

KORVU: THE BEGINNING
The prequel to The Wild One
Jai Ansuni was the first female Atapi sorcerer for thousands of years, but she dare not reveal it. However, when tribal sorcerer, Stacion Ansuni escalates the enmity between Atapi and Kumatan to an ominous level. Jai and her womb mate, Con, try to mitigate his atrocities but can two young Atapi, not even a score of years old, win against the powerful sorcerer?

THE WILD ONE
Sixteen year old Jai Cassidy thought she was finally free of her family until she is discovered by her other relatives…the ones that aren't human. Jai uses her natural perversity and cunning to escape their control, but catapults herself into the middle of a deadly feud between two alien races.

ATAPI SORCERESS
The sequel to The Wild One
Jai Cassidy is beginning her mission of reversing the decline of the non-humanoid Atapi. As a sorceress and an Atapi-Human hybrid, she is vehemently disliked by the male Atapi sorcerers and the humanoid rulers of Korvu. Her task is complicated by the treachery of a group of alien engineers, who are inciting insurrection and harsh reprisals.

THE TYMOREAN TRUST BOOK 1 - POWER RISING
The Tymorean Trust - When peace rules Tymorea - Peace reigns in the universe. Chosen to be the Advocates of the mystical and incorporeal Guardians of Peace, twins Tymos and Kryslie must first learn to control and use the power rising in them - or it will destroy them. On Tymorea, only the ruling Triumvirate Governors are powerful enough to guide the strong-willed alien-bred twins until they have mastered their power.

THE TYMOREAN TRUST BOOK 2 - GREAT ONES
The peace of the Guardian Planet, Tymorea, is in deadly peril. War there will create ripples of unrest and destruction throughout the settled universe. Tymos and Kryslie, still adolescents, have barely mastered their power and

Llaimos is still less than a year old, but they are the three chosen to be Advocates of the mystical Guardians of Peace, to safeguard the Tymorean Trust.

THE TYMOREAN TRUST BOOK 3 - RETURN TO EARTH

Even before the war on Tymorea, the Elders foresaw that Great Ones Tymos and Kryslie would have an imperative mission on Earth.

But as the Tymoreans prepare to build an Earthbase to support them, they discover that specifications for two vital protective shields are missing.

Now, nearly a century later, Tymos and Kryslie must find his work and build the generator before the base is found.

THE TYMOREAN TRUST BOOK 4 - EARTH MISSION

Just before their graduation from the prestigious WSRA Washington University, Tymos and Kryslie Ward deliberately disappear. The Great Ones have foreseen the capture and death of the new Tymorean missionaries and discovered that the leader of the Eastern Imperium plans to undermine the United World Nations. Tymos and Kryslie must protect their kin and prevent a potentially devastating world war.

THE TYMOREAN TRUST BOOK 5 – ALIEN CONTACT

Tymos and Kryslie Ward, hide their Tymorean intelligence and abilities while working as low ranked technicians at the WSRA's lunar base. When an alien ship arrives at Lunar One, pursued by a powerful enemy who will stop at nothing to get what he wants, only the two Tymorean Great Ones have the knowledge and abilities to overcome him, but to do so they must risk their sanity, and their souls.

THE TYMOREAN TRUST BOOK 6 – INVASION

Great Ones Tymos and Kryslie go to rescue the crew of Earth's first deep space mission – and discover that Ciriot space pirates have discovered Earth's location. When the Ciriot invade in force, the Great Ones reveal themselves so that Earth can gain vital help. However, Kryslie becomes the victim of Ciriot, who want to control her mind and make her betray the people of Earth.

TRICKS

Tom and Jo Dwyer had a reputation for playing tricks – and getting detention. They didn't seem to care about that, so long as they made their class laugh. That was until someone began to turn their tricks against them, and it was no longer funny.

SHORT STORIES:
GRAFFITI GIRL

Valerie has become known as "The Graffiti Girl" but she is more than just a street artist. She sees and paints life her way.
In Valkyrie, the second story, Valerie, blinded by an explosion, must learn to paint and see again.

GHOST WRITER

Edwina is a ghost with a mission - to find out why she died. Only to do so, she must first help another girl.

RATTLING CHAINS

I slammed the phone to my ear, "Colin! Where are you?" I was yelling.
"I haven't time for that. I need your help."
"What? Where?"
"Grab the chain, Hetty! Grab it, and don't let go."
"What chain? Colin? What chain?"
He was gone.

CRAZY TAILS

Three of these stories are based on real creatures I have known, but their names have been changed to protect the not so innocent. The incidents are real, the events happened, but the telling is tempered by nostalgia and the POV – that's where the fantasy comes in.
Spend some moments as a mouse, a possum, a cat and a rabbit.